Check My Pulse
For Love

By:
" Bleu Lyric"
Bryanna L. Foster

Check My Pulse For Love

Camren Blake sat in his dorm room with his girlfriend, Morgan Price. Camren was a senior at the University of San Francisco, California; Morgan was a senior as well. Camren was pre-med and Morgan majors in communication and minor in business. Camren watched as Morgan walked around his room touching his things, her peach dress reminded him of the first time they met. They were at a Frat party; she wore a dress with the same color and a pair of nude heels. He had offered her a strawberry Smirnoff that night which she had rejected because she was the driver for the night. He admired her for that, but that didn't stop him from pursuing her. That was two years ago and she still looks as breathtaking to this day.

"Are we still going to get something to eat? I'm hungry," Morgan asked as she played with his old baseball mitt. He had quit playing a year ago to focus on becoming a doctor although he did miss the game.

"I wanted to talk to you about something first," he said, patting the bed meaning for her to sit beside him.

She chortled. "You're always getting serious? Can we eat before you break some bad news to me?"

Camren looked down at the floor wondering if this was a good time, if ever, to tell her. He had to admit that after two years of dating he was still in love with this girl. She had his heart and he wasn't ready to take it back. "Nevermind, go ahead let's talk," she said as she sat down in my green bean bag chair across from where I was sitting on the bed.

"You know I love you right?" Camren asked her as he fidgeted with his hands.

"Are you joking? Or are you serious right now, Camren? Because my stomach ain't with your games today," she said with a roll of her honey brown eyes.

"I'm serious, Morgan, you are very special to me and you will always have a special place in my heart," he told her as he continued to look down at his hands nervously.

"What are you saying?" she asked him, she leaned forward.

"I'm saying' we should see other people," he said as he avoided eye contact.

"What?" she said with a frown.

"I'm 21-years-old, I'm going to be on my way to med school soon and I'm just not feeling the whole

2

commitment thing. I'm young, a relationship is just not what I need right now. I'll be spending what? Another four to seven years in school, this just isn't gonna work Morgan."

She sat back crossed her arms. "Are you cheating on me, Cam?" "What? No."

She got up and walked over to him, she turned his head to her. "Then what's all this bull you're throwing at me about not feeling a commitment."

He admired the way she handled situations, she would face it like it was instead of trying to avoid it. She was always willing to get to the root of the problem. This isn't what he was used to and why he desired to have her in his life.

"Like I said, I'll be too focused on school to be trying to juggle a relationship."

"Camren," she sort of whined. "Don't, baby, that makes this a whole lot harder," he said as he turned his head and continued to avoid eye contact for he felt tears welling up in his eyes already. "Can't we just talk about this?" He shrugged. "I don't know if talking will help, babe. "She sighed; her honey colored eyes had turned to a darker brown. She dabbed at the corners of her eyes with the pad of her middle finger.

"Since you are not willing to discuss this further then I guess this is it. Since you believe that being together this long is not worth breaking down and talking about then so be it," she said, her tone changing from sad to mellow. He looked down at the floor. "I'm not saying that I wouldn't be willing to do so, but that I don't think talking will provide change."

"Ok and I can't do anything but respect it. I'm going to excuse myself."

He didn't know what else to say to her, he had no words to assure her that breaking up would be better for them. He watched as she stood up and slowly exited his room. Watching her leave almost broke him, he almost got up and followed her and begged her to stay with him. He didn't want to picture her going back to her room crying on the shoulders of her roommates while they fed her words about how there's always someone else out there that would appreciate her. Part of that was true, she did deserve better than him.

Camren never stopped thinking about Morgan. There were days where he just wanted to call her and tell her his true feelings. To tell her the truth about his feelings for her, that letting her go was not the decision he wanted to make but had to make in order for both of them to grow.

He wanted her with his whole heart and knew in his heart that there was no other woman who could be who she was for him.

♥ Seven years later Camren is a doctor at St Vincent Carmel Hospital. He was one of the top Orthopedic surgeons in Indiana. Since his break up with Morgan he hadn't had a real relationship, there were little flings here and there but none held a candle to Morgan.

Camren quickly hopped into his black, RAM 1500 truck one Thursday morning; he was late for work which wasn't like him. He had a surgery that had run long the day before and he wasn't able to get home until early in the morning. He hadn't even brushed his teeth good enough this morning. He pulled into traffic hoping that it didn't make him even later. His phone rang; he reached for the phone making sure to keep his eyes on the road. He smiled when he read the name 'Kyles' on the caller ID.

"Yes Kyles?" he asked when he answered the phone. It was his best friend, Kylie Rivers. They have known each other for five years now. She was his person, the one he always talked to, the one who he confided in when he had an issue. He assumed she was calling to confirm their plans for the night.

"We still on for tonight?" she asked.

"So far," he sighed. "You better come; we haven't hung out in a while." "It is not my fault that broken collar bones and dislocated shoulders are more important," he teased as he looked in the rearview mirror at the beat up pickup truck honking in behind him.

"It is your fault, nobody told you to become a doctor." "You're just jealous that I make more money than you."

Camren heard Kylie laugh on the other end of the line. Kylie's a kindergarten teacher. He and she were always picking back and forth, she loved mentioning how much privilege he had being a doctor compared to her as a teacher.

"You're exactly right; doctors are just human beings, not gods. What do y'all do to get paid so much?"

"Besides saving lives? Nothing," Camren muttered as he backed into a parking space.

"Exactly my point." He chuckled and shook his head at her as he turned off the truck and got ready to get out. "Don't laugh at me, I am so serious."

"You're something else; I gotta go I'm at the hospital."
"See you at eight?" "It's a possibility."

"You know I don't take no for an answer."

"Bye."

He chuckled once more as he hung up. He was glad to have somebody like Kylie in his life, she was like the sister he never had. Having somebody he was comfortable enough to share his feelings with without them judging him was something he was really grateful for.

"Good Morning doctor," nurse, Debra, said to him as he went to the front desk to get his charts to start rounds.

"Good morning," he said as he wrote down in one of the charts.

"What do we have today doctor Blake?" Toby, a lanky guy with red hair and freckles, asked excitedly.

"Good Morning to you too, Toby," Camren said to him as he continued to scribble on the chart.

"Sorry doctor," Toby said as he dropped his head.

Toby was a nerdy guy, he didn't look no older than 26. Camren remembered being like Toby, getting into the job you know you love. Spending hours perfecting your craft and just excited for the next experience. The rest of the interns and their resident, Charlotte Kilts, filled in with Toby.

"Let's walk," Camren said to them. He handed Charlotte the charts and then he turned and started down the hall. They entered one of the patients' rooms.

"Tell me about the patient."

"Daniel Henry, 62 years old. Came in three days ago in need of a hip replacement," Charlotte said as she read off the charts. "His vitals are strong and he's ready for the surgery." "How are you feeling today Mr. Henry?" asked Camren. "Feeling pretty good son," the older man said with a warm smile.

His aura reminding Camren of the grandfather that raised him, he also had gray hair and he wore glasses.

"Doctor Blake, you're needed down in the ER right now," one of the nurses shouted as she ran into the room. "Doctor Kilts, take over here," Camren said. Then he rushed out of the room behind the nurse. "What's going on?" Camren questioned when he spotted Doctor Sophie standing in the middle of the Emergency Room.

Sophie looked up but didn't respond. There didn't look like there was an emergency. The emergency room was fairly calm, not the usual chaotic scene that he was accustomed to. Suddenly, the paramedics burst through the doors pushing a male patient in on the gurney. The patient was unconscious, his clothes were cut open and in disarray. Probably from when the paramedics had to get his heart going again.

"What do we have?" Camren asked one of the paramedics."22-year-old male, unconscious on the scene. Possible torn muscles in the knee."

"What's his name?" She didn't respond, just continued to move the patient. They were getting ready to transport the patient from the gurney to the bed.

"I'll ask again, have we identified the patient?"

Still no response. Camren helped the nurses push the patient into a private room; they closed the door behind them as well as the blinds and turned back to the patient.

"Doctor Blake, this is Devin Jordan," Samantha, our head neurologist, told Camren.

She was average height; she was a brunette and loved to wear red lipstick that made her dark eyes look darker.

"The basketball player?" Camren asked as he checked out the injury the patient obtained to his knee.

"Yes." "More like one of the greatest rookies to play the game," Sean exaggerated, checking the patient's ex pupils.

Sean was the usual pretty boy, he was always judged off his nice dirty blonde hair, perfect smile and full beard rather than his brains. "Could you take a look at his legs? His agent wants to know if he still has a career," Samantha said.

Camren took a look at the patient's leg. Devin had torn his anterior cruciate ligament (ACL) and it looked as if he was going to need surgery. Just as Camren was about to inform the other doctors of the news, a woman burst into the room.

"Ma'am, we're gonna need for you to leave," Samantha told her. Camren realized he recognized this woman, but from where? The memory wasn't clear as he looked at her face.

"Is he gonna be alright? Can he still play?" the woman asked obviously worried about the guy on the table. "Please, ma'am, leave the room," Sean told her.

"Nurse, could you escort this woman out?" Camren asked, ignoring the pint of familiarity that filled his senses for a moment.

The woman looked over at him and a moment of recollection crossed her face. Her big hazel eyes softened at the sight of the man before her as her lips quivered for a sentence.

It hit Camren suddenly. "Morgan?"

"We'll keep you updated," Sean told her as the nurse escorted her out of the room.

She nodded at Sean and then turned her gaze back over to Camren. It had been almost a decade since they had last seen or talked to each other.

What kind of fate brought them back into each other's lives? Seeing her brought back too many emotions. The room was suddenly feeling too warm for him.

"Who was that?" Sean asked Samantha. "She was hot."

Camren started to feel himself get upset; nobody talked about his Morgan like that. *'Your Morgan? It's been seven years since y'all last talked and you still think she's your Morgan?'* a part of him thought.

"Cam, you ok?" Sean asked with a concerned look, touching Camren's arm.

"Yeah, let me know when he's conscious," Camren said.

11

"Could you inform her on his status?" Samantha asked Camren.

"Yeah, sure," he said.

Camren felt reluctant to leave the room but he knew the sooner he faced Morgan, the better. He then removed his gloves and left the room. He made his way into the waiting area and saw Morgan pacing back and forth, talking on the phone. He halted in his stance and ran his eyes over her figure, drawing in every intricate detail. She looked good, different but good. She wore her brown hair in a short style and she had a certain glow about her. But those eyes...

He took a deep breath and then went over to her, ignoring the loud beating of his heart against his ribcage.

He walked to her and cleared his throat. "Excuse me." She stopped pacing, hung up and then looked over at him. "Your boyfriend's in critical condition and"- "Boyfriend? Devin's not my boyfriend."

"Oh, I'm sorry for assuming, but like I was saying, Mr. Jordan has a torn ACL that needs to be surgically repaired. As soon as he's conscious and settled in we will discuss the terms of his surgery."

"Ok." "Right now Dr. Reese and Dr. Wayne are working on Mr. Jordan, they will run a few tests to see if we're missing anything eternally and then we'll go from there."

She nodded, he nodded and then he turned to walk away.

"Devin," she called, suddenly making him freeze. He turned back around. "Excuse me?" "He likes to be called Devin." "Oh, ok."

"Will you be doing the surgery?"

"Yes unless you or Mr. Jordan decide otherwise."

"No, that's fine."

"Ok, well if you'll excuse me, I have to go."

*H*e couldn't stop thinking about Morgan; even throughout his work day running into her again was on his mind heavy. He had just made a repair to one of his patients' torn ligaments and he couldn't remember the process of how he completed the surgery, but judging by all hugs he received it was successful.

"So you're good at your job?" Morgan asked as she joined them in the waiting room while taking a swig from a cup of coffee.

"I guess you could say that," he said, finally able to snap out of his trance.

"Best Orthopedic surgeon in the state of Indiana," Morgan teased as if reading from an invisible notepad.

He removed his mask from around his neck, "You looked me up?"

She shrugged, "It's my job to know people."

The hope that she might have looked him up for other personal reasons deflated like a balloon.

"The life of an assistant to Devin Jordan, huh?" "Yep." "Never took you for the sports type."

She sipped her coffee, "It makes good pay. By the way, when can I see him?"

"He's still unconscious, more than likely the shock from the trauma. Body needs time to recover."

He turned to face her. "I will repair the torn tissue and he should be back to normal in the next six to nine months."

"Nine months? Wow."

"I said *six to nine months.*"

"Uh, I don't think he'll go for the surgery."

"What do you mean?"

"I mean Devin is a stubborn man, he might just refuse the surgery and just exercise his leg back to health."

"Healing without surgery is an option but that's not a good idea, his ACL is torn pretty badly. He can go to knee rehab but it's a possibility that exercise will hurt it more than help it. By adding pressure to an already strained ligament will injure him and cause more damage than before."

"We can tell him that but I doubt he'll listen to us."

He watched as she walked away. He took a deep breath; he had a patient he needed to check in on.

♥   When Camren arrived at the bar to meet with Kylie, he spotted her at the bar flirting with some guy. He was the same guy she usually goes for, cute face, nice body type, the type who she probably would see for a couple weeks and then dump him. He walked over to the bar and ordered a beer not wanting to interfere.

"Long day?" Camren heard Kylie whisper over his shoulder.

"Huh?" he asked, completely out of it.

She placed her hand on his shoulder. "Cam, are you ok?"

"Yeah, why you ask?"

The bartender placed the beer in front of Camren. He grabbed the beer and chugged down some of it.

"Because you're not here with me all the way."

"Just got a lot on my mind," he said, wiping at his mouth.

"You look spooked, like you seen a ghost," Kylie said jokingly, flipping her straight black hair.

Camren took several more gulps of his beer as he absent mindedly watched ESPN on the screen slightly to the left.

"Cam?" she said, sounding genuinely worried.

"What? I'm just thinking."

She sat her glass of Strawberry Daiquiri down and said, "About what?"

16

"Nothing," he said, shaking his head.

"Is it a patient with stage four cancer? A very complicated tumor? Somebody on life support?"

He shook his head. "No, nothing that serious, Kylie."

"You just called me Kylie, what's wrong?"

"That is your name," he said, sounding condescending as he sipped his beer.

"But you don't use it, tell me what's up?"

He drank the rest of his beer and then asked the bartender for another.

"You remember my ex from college?"

"Which one?"

Camren glared at her and she threw her hands up in surrender.

"Fine, the cheerleader you dated all throughout college? The same one that you came crying into my cafe that one windy afternoon," she asked as she sipped her Daiquiri.

"It was not windy, but yea."

"What about her?" she asked, taking a seat beside me once the gentleman that was there previously left.

"I saw her today," he said, playing with his bottle.

Her eyebrows raised. "What happened?"

"Her client, Devin Jordan, was my patient."

She gasped and swiveled on the stool. "My husband's in the hospital?"

"No, Devin's in the hospital."

She sucked her teeth. "Her client?"

"Yes, she's his assistant or agent. Something along those lines."

"Oh, how's Devin?"

"He has a torn ACL and I think surgery is his best option."

"Did you and Morgan talk?"

He finished off the his beer. "Not really."

As if reading Camren's mind the bartender brought him another beer. Camren grabbed it and began to gulp it down as well.

"So y'all saw each other but no words were exchanged?"

"Yep," he said with a nod of his head.

The room erupted into loud cheering, one of the teams from the NHL game showing on another TV. Camren noticed a woman with long brown skin and peach colored skin at the end of the bar making eye contact with him, she smiled at him but for some reason he didn't have the energy to give more than just a faint smile.

He noticed Kylie shaking her head at him, then she said, "What did she look like?"

"She's still as beautiful as she was seven years ago, if not even more. Her hair was in a bob cut that was still long enough to touch her shoulders. Eyes still a honey color and her skin was so smooth-looking."

Kylie turned her head to the side and looked at him weirdly. "You still have feelings."

"I don't know," he asked as he sipped his beer.

"You do, it's been nearly a decade and you still talk about her as if you're reading from a book."

"She was my first love, Kyles."

"And I can tell you still have those feelings for her."

Kylie was right, he did still have feelings for Morgan. Not only was she his first true love but she was his only. He would never be able to love any other girl the same way he loved her, he loved her so much he had bought her a ring. He had never told anybody about the ring, he still had it sitting in his drawer next to his socks. Every time he goes into that drawer he picks it up and reminisces. He couldn't bring himself to get rid of it. After all these years of trying to rid himself of these feelings maybe this was now fate, maybe destiny was bringing her back to him so that they can rekindle the love that they once shared.

♥   The next morning Camren did his regular rounds at the hospital going around checking in on his patients. He and other doctors stood in Devin's room waiting to read off his charts.

"Talk to me," Camren told Toby.

"Devin Jordan, 22-year-old male professional basketball player. He was rushed into the ER with a mild concussion and a torn ACL," Toby said.

"We kept him monitored over night to track his progress. He awoke from his coma early this morning," one of the interns named Kolbe said.

"How you doing, Mr. Jordan?" Camren asked Devin.

"Pretty good, just ready to go," Devin said.

"You're looking good," Camren said as he checked Devin's eyes with his light.

"So when can we get to signing those discharge papers?" Devin asked.

"We would like to take another look at your knee again, maybe run a few more scans on your head to check your brain for any damages."

"Could we make it quick? Basketball is calling my name."

Camren had of some his team dismissed to go check on the other patients and made sure to schedule a CT for Devin. He then checked Devin's ears and his reflexes.

"Can we ask what you were doing at the time of the accident?" Camren asked Devin.

"I was playing basketball," Devin grumbled.

"He was playing on the black tops with no rules with some street thugs," Morgan said as she entered the room.

"And then what? You came down on your leg wrong?" asked Camren.

"More like someone else came down on his leg trying to purposely ruin his career," she said as she came and stood beside the bed.

"Would you calm down and stop being so dramatic, Morgan?" Devin said. "Doc, how do you two know each other?"

A look of panic crossed Morgan's face. "Uh, we went to school together."

"You went to school with one of the best Orthopedic surgeons, I'm proud of you, Morgan," Devin said.

She rolled her eyes at him. Cam chuckled and shook his head. But he couldn't help but wonder what type of relationship Devin and Morgan had, even though it wasn't his business.

"Mr. Jordan, I would like to talk to you about your leg," Camren said to Devin, desperately needing to change the subject.

"Do you know a good knee rehab facility back in Denver?" Devin asked.

"I believe surgery is one of your best options."

"There's always another option, Dr. Blake."

"But surgery is your best one."

"I appreciate your concern, Dr. Blake, but I don't want the surgery."

"You're more likely to recover better with the surgery," Doctor Charlotte interrupted.

"And Dr. Blake is one of the best," Toby said.

"I understand, but it's my leg and I know me the best"

Camren sighed in annoyance, "That's your decision, I wish you luck with your recovery."

Devin nodded his thanks. Camren left the room, he has had patients that were stubborn but he had never seen any trying to purposely ruin the chances.

Devin was willing to make his leg worse in order to play ball.

Camren was in the cafeteria looking for a place to sit and eat his lunch when he spotted Morgan sitting alone, he went over to her.

"May I?" he asked her.

She looked up from her phone at him and motioned for him to take a seat.

"Hey," he said as he sat down.

"Hi," she said as her fingers typed away at her phone.

"I hope I'm not interrupting anything."

"Nope, you just saved me from continuously rejecting guys in here. I was actually thinking about you," she said as she typed her last words and then put her phone down on the table.

He was surprised to hear that, he raised an eyebrow at her.

"I was meaning to talk to you about Devin."

He nodded. "Oh."

"I told you he was very headstrong, he dislikes hospitals for some reason. Whenever he's sick he has the doctor come to him."

Camren grabbed his apple and bit into it. "He's a grown man, he can make his own decisions, even if they could possibly complicate his life."

She looked down at his tray, he had a turkey sandwich with a side salad, an apple and a bottle of water.

"On a diet?" she asked.

"Not at all, when I became a doctor I started eating healthier. Don't get me wrong, I enjoy a good burger sometimes, but I'm trying to watch my figure."

They both laughed. God, he still so enjoyed the sound of her laughter. Seeing her smile with her perfect pearly white teeth and to see the color fill her cheeks after laughing too hard gave him life.

"How about it?" she asked.

"How about what?"

He realized he was so deep in thought he hadn't heard what she had just asked of him.

"How about you join Devin and me for dinner sometime next week? You could explain the surgery to him in a surrounding that's comforting to him."

Camren picked up his sandwich. "What good would that do?"

"You could change his mind."

"Much easier said than done," he said before biting into his sandwich.

"It's doable."

"How do I know it's not a complete waste of my time?"

"You'll just have to take a chance," she said with a shrug.

He thought about it for a moment, contemplating this suggestion. She watched as he gave it some thought, making sure to smirk at him. She knew he loved a challenge and that he would be willing to give it a try.

"And what do I get out of this?" he asked. Then he took another bite of his sandwich.

"A free meal," she said with a smile.

He smiled back. "Then I'll go."

26

"Great, here's my number," she said as she reached in her handbag and pulled out a card.

"I'll give you a call."

"You do that," she said, teasingly.

Camren asked Kylie to join him to dinner because he didn't trust himself not to stare at Morgan the whole time. They sat in the small dimly lit restaurant in the corner next to the window. It was late in the evening so the sun was down and night was slowly settling in.

"Why am I here?" Kylie asked Camren as they sat waiting for Devin and Morgan.

"Because you love me, Devin's coming *and* you're getting a free meal," he told her as he messed with the buttons on his blue polo shirt.

"Reverse that, the meal, my husband and then you." "Husband?" "Yes, Devin is my husband. I have watched all his games since high school, he even autographed my shirt. Which I have yet to wash by the way."

He rolled his eyes at her. "And why wasn't I invited to the wedding?"

"We eloped," she said as she ate the bread sticks that were provided for them.

Camren burst into laughter. That's why he loved her, she was crazy and wasn't afraid to embrace it.

"Sorry we're late, as you can see I'm considered handicap," Devin said as he and Morgan made their way over to the table.

"It's no problem," Camren said as he stood to his feet. "Everybody wants to be considered handicap just so they can get that parking spot, but not many want to actually be handicap."

Devin and Camren laughed together before Devin took Camren hand with the hand that wasn't holding his crutches. Then Camren glanced at Morgan who was standing just behind Devin, he noted that her hands were pale and assumed it was from clutching her purse too tight.

"Who's this beauty?" Devin asked, eyeing Kylie.

"Kylie Rivers," she said, trying to hide the big grin on her face.

"Nice to meet you," he said, taking her hand softly.

"You as well," she said, staring into his eyes. The moment they shared was brief but intense, Camren and Morgan watch their interaction.

"Kylie, this is Morgan Price," Camren introduced them, interrupting the moment.

"Oh," Kylie said. "Nice to meet you. Heard alot about you."

"Nice to meet you too," Morgan said.

Camren gave Kylie the side eye indicating that he didn't want her to go into that at this moment. Then everybody took their seats, they sat at a square table, Kylie sat to Camren's right facing the door and Devin sat next to Morgan on her left.

"I'm a big fan," Kylie told Devin.

"Aren't we all?" Morgan said sarcastically.

"I especially enjoyed your game against the Clippers. You were on fire, I loved that behind the back pass to Kevin Scott," Kylie said.

Everybody looked at her in astonishment, including Camren. He and Kylie have watched the super bowl and play offs together at his place but she was usually on her phone most of the time.

"So you *are* a fan?" Devin said.

"I told you I was," she said with a slight shrug.

"I'm glad to hear that, maybe I could provide tickets to the next game," Devin said as he slowly leaned on the table to touch her hand.

"That would be great," Kylie said, smiling back like a school girl, "When will you be back?"

Camren and Morgan looked at each other with the same worried expression.

"We don't know for sure, but I'd like to think I'll be back for playoffs," Devin said.

"Oh ok, I'll be looking forward to it."

"So, how long have you two known each other?" Devin asked both Camren and Kylie. Kylie looked over at Camren. "Uh, six years now." "How sweet?" Morgan said with a hint of mockery.

"I guess so," Camren said. "So what's it like knowing a doctor?" Devin asked. "It has it perks, I get free doctor visits," Kylie said, playfully hitting Camren on his arm.

They all laughed, but Morgan's laugh didn't reach her eyes. Camren wondered what was bothering her. Did she see Kylie as a threat? He watched as she sipped from her glass of water, slightly frowning at Kylie whenever she talked.

"Let's talk business, shall we?" Camren asked.

"We haven't ordered yet, Cam," Kylie said.

"I pre-ordered our meals, everybody enjoys salmon," Devin said.

"I'm allergic-" "She's allergic," Camren said at the same time Morgan spoke.

Both Devin and Kylie looked from Camren to Morgan. Kylie smiled a knowing smile at Camren.

"I see you still remember," Morgan said to Camren. Camren nodded as he kept a straight face. How could he forget when she was the only thing on his mind for these past years? "I always forget," Devin said.

"It's ok," Morgan said as she gently touched his arm. Camren saw the exchange and couldn't help but look away. "Y'all must've been really close friends," Devin said to Camren.

"We were, real close," Camren said, looking at Morgan.

Kylie elbowed him, that's when he noticed his pager was going off. There was an emergency at the hospital. "I gotta go," Camren said.

"Hospital?" Kylie asked.

He nodded as he got up. She grabbed her purse and got up, she knew the routine. After years of being his friend she was accustomed to interruptions from the hospital, plus they rode together in her car.

"Reschedule?" Camren asked Devin.

"Of course, I'll have Morgan call you," Devin said.

"Sounds great." Then he and Kylie hurriedly exited the restaurant.

Camren had recently gotten home

from the hospital and finished up a long hot shower and started to pack an overnight bag because he had a long surgery ahead of him. He had a femur surgery on a 19 year old boy who's an avid skater. At that moment his phone rang.

"Hello?" he said, answering it as he continued to pack. "Dr. Blake?" the female on the other line said. "This is he." "It's Ms. Price or Morgan," she said. Camren noted that she sounded like she was driving in the car, he could hear the sound of the tires on the road.

He paused and stopped. "What can I help you with, Ms. Price?"

"You wanted to reschedule our meeting."

"Ah yes I did.

"How's tomorrow?"

"I'm doing a femur surgery. How about Friday?" he asked as he looked at the calendar on his phone," he said, putting her on speaker.

"Busy," she said.

"Sounds like we have a problem. How about you come over and we'll check each other's calendars?"

She hesitated. "I don't know about that."

"It's just me, Morgan."

"Where do you live?" she asked with a puff.

He gave her the address to his condo, she told him she would arrive in the next 20 minutes and then they hung up. He was in the kitchen packing some food for the surgery when he heard a knock at the door. He answered the door forgetting he was shirtless until he opened the door and Morgan's mouth fell open. Her eyes went to the tattoo on his chest that said her name in Japanese. She remembered the first time she saw it, she was intrigued as to what it said. When she had asked he had replied that it was her name.

"Ms. Price?" he said, silently laughing.

"Uh, I …" She cleared her throat, "I would- could you go put on a shirt?"

He chuckled. "Sure, come on in."

He went over and grabbed his shirt off the back of the couch.

"Do you have a date for me?" he asked as he put on the shirt.

She got her calendar out of her handbag. "How's the ninth?"

He looked at the calendar nailed to the wall in the kitchen. "Uh … oh, can't I have two hip replacement surgeries to perform. How about the tenth?"

"Seven o'clock good for you?"

"Yep."

She put her calendar away. "Ok, good. We'll be in touch." She threw her bag over her shoulder and made her way over to the door to leave.

"Penelope," he said before she reached the door.

She stopped her movement. "Never thought I would hear you say that again."

34

"Never thought I would get the chance to say it again."

He came in behind her, she looked good in her tan pants suit. It fit her body nicely, extenuating her curves. He could smell peaches on her, a smell he was all too familiar with.

"It's been too long, Morgan," he breathed.

"What are you doing?"

She was just as affected by his existence as he was by hers. He leaned in close, about to wrap his arms around her when her phone started to ring. She moved away and quickly removed her phone from her bag.

"Hello?" she said, putting her ear to the phone. "Yes … I'm on my way." Then she hung up.

"I understand, you gotta go," he said, taking a couple steps back.

He watched her as she made her way out of his apartment in a hurry, it reminded him of when she walked out of his dorm room seven years ago. He took a deep breath, trying to get all of his emotions under control.

His heart felt as if it was going to beat out of his chest because the last time Morgan walked out on him like that she never came back. He looked over at the calendar on the wall, that was his reminder that she was coming back. That they were going to see each other again.

Camren didn't know what had come over him. He didn't know why he had come onto Morgan the other night. He couldn't contain the feelings that had consumed him at that moment. It was just that whenever he was near her the feelings he had back in college came back. Thank God her phone had rang when it did because any longer in that apartment with her and they would've done something they shouldn't have.

♥   He was out at a party with one of his old college buddies, Ryan Alexander. He used to be a linebacker in college, but gave up the ball for a career as an otolaryngologist.

"Are you gonna sit here like a bump on a log? Or are you gonna dance?" Ryan asked Camren.

"I'm just gonna take it easy tonight," Camren said as he sipped on his beer.

"Ok, but there's some smoking hot babes in here and if one of them asks you to dance, you are going to dance with her."

Camren laughed and shook his head at Ryan. 15 minutes later Camren was still standing around drinking his beer. He couldn't stop thinking about Morgan, he was anxious to see her face again.

"You look like a loner, suga."

Camren glanced over his shoulder and saw a woman standing behind him. "Nah, my friend is out there dancing."

"And why aren't you out there dancing too, baby?" she asked as she played with her black hair.

She gave him '45-year-old hooker from the 80s' vibes with the way she spoke to him. But the amount of alcohol she had consumed to this point could've had some effect on her speech.

"Not really in the mood to dance."

"That makes you and the little lady over there staring at you."

He looked in the direction she was pointing at and saw a lady sitting across from the bar wearing a black fitted dress sipping a cocktail.

"Excuse me," he told her before making his way over to the lady.

"Mmmmm," she said grinning.

He made his way over to the brunette that had been watching him. She had turned her head as if he hadn't caught her looking.

"Would you care to dance?" he asked her.

"No thanks, I don't dance," she said, not even looking at him.

He knew exactly who this woman was. She was the same woman that made his heart race just by speaking, the same woman that had brought a smile to his face since he first met her.

He sat his beer down on the table next to them. "That's a shame because I know you like to dance, Penelope."

Her head popped up. "Camren?"

"Finally recognized me after staring for an hour, huh?" he said with a smile. "The girl I remember used to be a real fireball out on the dance floor."

"Things change," she said as she nervously stirred her straw in her cocktail.

"Yeah, but dancing is always in your heart."

He grabbed her hand and began pulling her towards the dance floor. She sat her glass down and allowed him to pull her along.

"I don't dance anymore," she said.

"Tell that to someone who doesn't know you, Morgan," he whispered in her ear.

She was stiff at first, but started laughing and shuffling her feet when the second song came on. This was their first night at the party all over again, them on the dance floor laughing and having a good time.

"See, I told you," he said to her.

She smiled as they moved to the music. When a slow jam came on Morgan's eyes widened with panic.

"Can I get you a drink?" he asked, deciding to put her mind at ease.

"Yes please?" she said. Then they walked off the dance floor.

Camren saw the relief on her face. As they were walking Camren saw Devin sitting at a table with a few guests, then he led them over to the table.

"Dr. Blake, it's funny seeing you here," Devin said when he saw them.

"I try to get out," Camren said. "How's the leg?"

"It's fine, still hurts at times."

"Oh ok, you got some medicine for that?"

Devin smirked. "Yes sir."

"Ok great, I'll see you guys later."

"Wait a minute, doc. Guys this is the man who saved my life," Devin said as he introduced Camren to the guys beside him.

"What's up," they said to Camren.

"Good to meet you all," Camren said.

"Did Morgan invite you to the party?" asked Devin.

Camren looked over at Morgan who was trying to hide her face by playing with her hair. "Party?"

"Um, I'm sure Dr. Blake is very busy," Morgan said.

"Hey, babe," a guy with blonde hair said as he came up to Morgan and kissed her on the cheek.

"Oh hey," she said.

"This is Morgan's boyfriend, Tyler," Devin said.

Boyfriend?

"Nice to meet you, I'm Camren, I'm a friend of Morgan's," Camren said as they shook hands.

Camren gave the guy a once over, the guy had brown eyes and a square jaw. He wasn't built like the rest of the guys that were with Devin, he was taller and pale.

"Oh ok, nice to meet you," said Tyler.

"So are you busy tomorrow, Dr. Blake? Because we would like for you to attend our party," Devin said.

"Actually, no, my schedule's free," Camren said.

"Great, Morgan, you can give him the details, right? You can even bring a date."

"Sure," she said through gritted teeth.

Camren and Kylie pulled up at what seemed like a mini mansion, apparently it was the location of the party. Camren told Kylie about his invite to the party and she invited herself, said she it was her lucky day to see Devin for a second time. Camren shook his head at her but knew that he would have invited her to be his "wingman" anyways.

"How do I look?" Kylie asked Camren as they stood on the doorstep of the house.

"You look fine, Kyles," Camren told her.

"We're going to see my husband, I have to look perfect," she said as she ran her hand over her light green sundress.

"Would you stop it?" he asked in an agitated tone.

"Ok, ok, I'm good, go ahead and ring the bell," she said with sass.

Camren rang the doorbell, a few seconds later, Melissa, Morgan's younger sister answered the door. Her once brown hair was now touched up with blonde highlights. She had it pulled back into a tight ponytail and brown eyes with gold flecks.

She had grown up more since the last time Camren had seen her, she was now a young woman instead of the innocent teen he once knew. "Melissa?" he said with furrowed eyebrows. "So you're a doctor now?" she asked.

"Yeah."

"Always knew you would amount to nothing," she said sarcastically with a smile. "I'm sure you did," he said, sharing the same smile.

She stepped out and hugged him. "It's so good to see you, Cam." "You too, Mel."

"Come on in, everybody's out back," she said, motioning them inside. "Thank you," he said as he and Kylie followed her inside. "This is my friend, Kylie Rivers."

"Melissa," she said as she waved at Kylie. "Hi," Kylie said. "Dr. Blake, so glad you two could make it," Devin said as Camren and Kylie made their way out into the back with everybody else.

"Thanks for inviting us," Camren said.

Tyler sat beside Morgan on a sofa with a little girl wearing a tiara with purple jewels sitting in the middle. The yard was decorated in red ribbon, there was a happy birthday sign above the table with a matching red cloth covering it, and there was a pile of presents on this table.

The young girl had a hint of green in her eyes, and she was missing a tooth on the bottom row of her mouth. She had her hair braided back into two big braids.

"Can I get you both something to drink?" Devin asked them.

"No thanks," Camren said.

"Uncle DJ, can I go swimming?" the little girl asked Devin.

"No you may not, not until the rest of your guests arrive," Morgan told her.

"But I'm hot," the girl whined.

Devin put his arm around the girl's neck. "How about you go get some ice cream from the kitchen?"

"She hasn't even eaten any real food yet," Morgan fussed at him.

"It's the girl's birthday, let her live," he said.

Morgan rolled her eyes at him. Camren chuckled at their bickering.

"Go get you some ice cream," Devin told April.

"Yay!" April said as she got up and made her way towards the house.

"Don't run, April!" Morgan called after her.

"Ok!" April said. Then she went inside.

"I'll go help her," Tyler told Morgan as he stood up.

Camren watched him as he walked by, he wondered what Morgan saw in him. I mean Camren had to admit that the guy was well put together, he looked like he had things going for himself. He still didn't like him, especially not for Morgan.

"She's so beautiful," Kylie said about the little girl. "Thank you, she looks just like her mother," Devin said. "She's not yours?" Kylie asked him.

"Oh no, I don't have any kids." "Yet," Melissa said as she brought a pitcher of lemonade out and sat it on one of the tables. "You hush," Devin told her.

"Are you sure we can't get you two anything?" Morgan asked Camren and Kylie.

"I'll take a glass of lemonade," Kylie said.

"I gotta go get the glasses," Melissa said. Then she went back into the house.

"Where's the bathroom?" Camren asked. "There's one down the hall, first door on the left when you go inside," Devin told him.

"Thanks," Camren said as she got up and went inside.

♥ Camren couldn't help but wonder who the little girl belong to if she wasn't Devin's. Was that Tyler dude the father? Camren thought as he washed his hands in the bathroom. Then who would be her mother? Couldn't be Melissa's, could it?

"Is it true you're gonna help Uncle DJ get all better?" April asked him as she and another little girl with reddish-brown braided back stood outside the bathroom.

"Uh, yes, I'm helping your Uncle get all better," he told her.

"Good because I don't like him on *crunches*," she said. "Me either," the other little girl said. Camren chuckled at their mispronunciation of the word crutches.

"Mommy says that you're a doctor," April said. "Which one's your mommy?" he asked.

He watched as she pointed to the backyard, he got down to their level and saw that she was pointing at Morgan through the window.

Now it was making sense as to why Morgan was so protective over the girl, because she was her daughter. He should've seen it before she had her mother's smile. So did that make Tyler the father?

"That's right, I'm a doctor," Camren told her.

"Cool, can we see your stethoscope? I wanna hear my heartbeat," the other little girl asked.

"What are your names?" Camren asked.

"I'm April and this is Courtney," April introduced the both of them.

"Well April, I'm sorry to tell you that I left it at home," he said, chuckling at her.

"Ah man," they both said before pouting.

Camren head footsteps coming from behind him followed Morgan's voice saying, "Are you girls bothering Mr. Blake?"

"No ma'am," April said as she and the other little girl shook their heads.

"We were just chatting," Camren said, looking at her over his shoulder.

"Why don't you girls go change and then join the other girls in the pool?" Morgan asked.

"Yes ma'am," they said then went inside the bathroom.

"Morgan," Camren said in a stern tone.

She closed her eyes. "Yes?" "How old is she?" he asked as he stood to his feet

"five." Morgan replied

He calculated the months, there was no way he could be the father. He was relieved but also a little saddened. He had once imagined himself and Morgan having kids together. He opened his mouth to speak but she spoke first.

"I gotta go help set out the food," she said. Then she twirled around.

He grabbed her wrist, keeping her from going. "Morgan."

He had so many questions whirling around in his mind for her. She looked up at him, they shared an intense gaze.

He took a step towards her, hoping that getting closer to her would make the increasing ache in his body finally cease. That's when the bathroom door opened, they quickly moved away from each other.

"Mommy, when can we eat the cake?" April asked Morgan as she stood before them in a turquoise bathing suit.

Camren ran a hand through his hair, he was still struggling to wrap his head around the news that Morgan was a mother.

"Soon, sweetie," Morgan told her.

"Where's the birthday girl?" Morgan's mother, Kathy, called out as the front door opened and closed.

"Grammie!" April shouted. Then she and the little girl ran off. Camren and Morgan looked at each other, then went their separate directions. He made his way back outside, "Where've you been?" Kylie asked him as he returned and sat down beside her.

"Bathroom," he said. "Uh-huh," she said with disbelief.

"So glad you could be here, ma," Morgan told Kathy.

Kathy and Morgan had the same eye color and nose, Kathy's hair was lighter from getting older. Kathy had a way about her that made the hardest thug on the block become a puddle of sap. "Wouldn't miss it for the world," Kathy said as they hugged.

"Nice to see you again, Mrs. Price," the blonde haired guy said to her. "Same to you, Tyler," she said lethargically. "Hello, Kathy," Devin said to her

"Hello, Devin, and please call me Mrs. Price," Kathy told him bluntly. "Alright! What kind of party is this? Where's the cake? Where's the party favors? Where's the- Camren?" He smiled at her. "Hello, Mrs. Price."

"Oh my God," she said with a huge smile as she rushed over to him and hugged him. "It's been so long."

She grabbed his face and kissed his right cheek. He was always a big fan of Morgan's mother, and she was the mother he always longed for.

Camren didn't have much of a mother figure after his parents passed away in that car wreck when he was only 8 years old, leaving his grandmother to raise him.

"It's good to see you too, Mrs. Price."

"You can call me Kathy," she told him. "How've you been?"

"Good, how about you?"

She grinned from ear to ear. "Wonderful."

"Good to hear, you look it."

She playfully hit his arm. "Oh stop it. This your girlfriend?"

"No ma'am, this is my friend, Kylie."

Kylie stood to her feet and offered her hand. Camren looked over and saw Morgan's face relax.

"Nice to meet you, darling," Kathy said to Kylie as they shook hands.

"Same to you," Kylie said.

"Did you bring me something, Grammie?" April asked Kathy as she floated on the surface in the pool.

"I sure did, your-"

"Poppie's here!" Morgan's father, Mike, announced as he came out back carrying a large box with a bow. From the imaging on the box it was assumed that it was a bike inside.

Camren sat down, ducking his head. He hoped Mike hadn't seen him yet. Unlike Kathy, Mike didn't welcome Camren with open arms, he always gave Camren a hard time. It was like Mike had a personal vendetta against him. When Camren was getting serious about Morgan, Mike threatened Camren into leaving her alone for the best of them both.

"Poppie!" April shouted as she got out of the pool and ran towards Mike.

"April don't!" Morgan warned her.

"It's alright, it's just a bit of water," Mike told Morgan as he hugged April.

"Nice to see you again, Mr. Price," Tyler told Mike.

"Tyler, my favorite son-in-law," Mike said as they shook hands.

"Let's go," Camren whispered to Kylie.

"What?" she asked.

"Please, let's go," he begged.

Kylie rolled her eyes but didn't ask any question. Camren grabbed her hand as they slowly tip-toed their way out, hoping to go unseen.

"Where you going, Dr. Blake?" April asked, blowing their cover.

Camren silently groaned as he and Kylie stopped in his tracks. Now Mike could see him and he could hear it now. He could hear Mike's disappointment as he realized that Camren was back around.

"He has a patient," Kylie said, coming to his rescue.

"Well, well, well," Mike said when he saw Camren.

Camren cringed at his voice. Mike was a big guy, in length and weight. He was the average father, he had a beer gut with peppered hair and goatee.

"Hello, Mr. Price," Camren said with a frown.

"Hello, Camren."

"Just came by to give my best wishes, show my face."

"Well now you can leave," Mike said bluntly.

"Mike!" Kathy said with disdain.

"It's alright, Mrs. Price, like she said, I have a patient that needs my help," Camren said.

Then he and Kylie made their way out the house and to his car.

The whole car ride Camren was quiet, he was grateful that Kylie didn't push the conversation, he knew he owed her an explanation for leaving so abruptly but he just wasn't ready to open that wound open again.

Camren was working himself hard at the hospital trying to erase what had happened at April's party from his mind. He hadn't really slept in a couple hours, but he did manage to find time in between patients to get a cat nap in. He was going to give a consult for one of the cardiologists on a patient that was experiencing mild chest pains after a bad fall. He was turning the corner when Morgan's voice stopped him. He turned around to see her in a nice tan, peach and navy striped dress, running towards him.

"Morgan? What are you doing here?" he asked her.

"I came … to apologize … for the party," she said in between breaths.

He moved away from the elevator. "There's no need to."

"There is because I know there was no patient."

I gave her a look of confusion. "What do you mean?"

She placed her hand on her hips and gave me a look that said, 'Ha, try again.' I sighed and said, "Ok, maybe there wasn't a patient at the time, but my feelings weren't hurt."

"You've changed, Camren," she said as she tilted her head to the side.

"In a good or bad way?" he asked, raising an eyebrow.

"You've matured so much, and now you're a doctor."

"Me? What about you? You've got a five-year-old and a career managing the life of a superstar."

It's been seven years and Camren is still stuck on her and what they had. He wondered how she had been able to move on so easily. Had she really dropped all feelings she once had for him?

"Just doing what any mother would do."

"And you're doing great at it."

She smiled at him "Thank you, she reminds me so much of her father sometimes."

"And who is her father?" "Have I met the guy?"

Her face dropped. "What?"

"Who's April's father? Was it that guy from the party? I wasn't completely sure if you guys were serious about each other or not," Camren said, prying.

"I ...uh, I-"

"Dr. Blake, we need you!" Samantha said as she ran passed them towards the elevator.

"What is it?" he asked.

"Seven-year-old, head injury to the back of the head. Slipped and fell while running by the pool."

"April!" Morgan cried.

"You don't know that," he told her.

"April always runs by the pool."

The elevator doors opened and they all got onto the elevator and rode it down to the ER, where a resident and two interns were working on the little girl.

"Move back!" Camren said as he and Samantha rushed in.

"April!" Morgan shouted as she began to bawl her eyes out.

One of the male nurses had to catch her from falling straight to the floor.

"I need four pints of blood, what blood type is she?" Camren asked Morgan.

She didn't respond, she just cried and watched April's face.

"Morgan!" I yelled to her.

She sniffed. "She's B positive."

"And you are?"

"A neg."

"Blood transfusion is our best option," Samantha said as they tried to get a handle on all the blood that Morgan was losing.

"Yes, but we're running out of time."

April was still losing blood, then she started to code.

"She's coding, paddles!" he shouted.

One of the nurses pushed over the cart and handed the paddles to him.

"Clear!" he said. Then he pressed the paddles against April's tiny chest.

Still no sign of a heartbeat. He did it again.

"Charge to 200!"   Still nothing. "Again!"

This time there was a pulse, Camren sighed with relief but there was no time for celebration. He had to do a transfusion before April ran out of time. Camren jumped into action.

"Let's get her up to surgery asap for a blood transfusion, we'll need a lot of blood so somebody call for blood. Let's move it people, call ahead and get a, OR ready," Camren shouted out orders as he began transporting April.

Camren and his colleges were able to get her bleeding under control and were about to get her stable. She had lost a good bit of blood but there was no sign of brain damage. Camren had just left the operating room, he rubbed at his tired eyes. I saw Morgan sitting beside a sleeping Tyler in the waiting area, when she saw him she got up and moved over to him.

"How's she doing? How's my baby? Did you save her?" Morgan asked Camren after the surgery.

"She's fine, the surgery went well, she's a tough girl," he told her.

"Thank you," she told him.

"Don't thank me, thank Dr. Reese."

She started crying, he felt the need to bring her in close to console her. So he did, he grabbed her and hugged her.

"She's gonna be fine," he reassured her as he pat her back, "If she complains about back pain, if there's blood in her urine, chills, fainting or dizziness, if she runs a fever, if she has any pain or her skin flushes then that's normal."

"Ok," Morgan said, sniffling.

"Want me to wake him?" Camren asked, referring to Tyler, who was still sleeping soundly.

"No, between me fussing at myself and my parents constantly fussing at me, I just can't do it. I just need to see my daughter," she said, breaking down once again.

"It is not your fault, you do all you can as a parent and that's the best you can do."

"I should've been there to stop her."

"I remember one time my mother told me, 'Don't climb that tree, Camren, don't climb that tree!'. Me being a kid I climbed the tree anyways, I ended up falling and breaking my arm. But I never climbed a tree again."

"Kids will be kids, I get that. It's my job as a parent to make sure she's ready for the real world and she can't do that if she doesn't even reach teen years."

"She's fine, Morgan, don't psych yourself out. Accidents happen and April is doing just fine. We both know you do what's best for April now is your love and support."

Tears fell down her cheeks, he pulled her off to the side where there weren't a lot of eyes to see her tears. Once out of sight he continued to hug her until her tears subdued. They stayed like that for about five minutes, it was a perfect moment. Him holding her while she cried on his chest. His pager started going off suddenly and she pulled back drying her eyes.

"I'm sorry," Camren said, looking at his pager.

"Go," she said.

"You gon' be alright?"

"I'll be fine," she said with a nod.

♥ Kylie was pushing one of her students on the swings during recess, the little girl, Abbey, was smaller than the other kids and was constantly bullied. Kylie made it routine to push the young girl on the swings so she wouldn't be alone.

"Thank you, Ms. Rivers," Abbey said.

"You're welcome," Kylie said. Then she went over to join the other teachers while Abbey chose another part of the playground to play on.

"The relationship you have with that little girl is adorable," one other the other teachers named Jane said to Kylie.

"Thank you," Kylie said as she sat down beside another teacher named Hector.

"I feel bad for her when the other kids make fun of her, I fuss at them when they do," said Hector.

"I used to be one of them," Kylie said.

"Getting bullied?" asked Hector

"No, bullying," Kylie said. Then they all laughed.

After school Kylie was waiting with Abbey for Abbey's mother to show up. Her mother always showed up late because she couldn't get off work early enough to be here at the required time for all car riders.

"What did you eat for dinner last night?" Kylie asked Abbey as they played tic-tac-toe on a small notepad.

"Sloppy Joe, mom said it was our new special meal of the week," Abbey said as she marked on the notepad.

"That's good, I like sloppy Joe too," Kylie said as she took her turn marking the paper.

"How sweet," Devin said from behind Kylie.

She asked as she whipped around to face him. "Where'd you come from?"

"I've been standing here for a little while." "Long enough to see our interaction?"

He nodded as he moved closer to them. She noticed that he was using his crutches at the moment, but he did have a slight limp. Abbey looked between Devin and Kylie trying to figure who he was to Kyle.

"It's nice of you to stay after hours," he said.

"Just doing my duty as her educator," Kylie said with a shrug as she started up a new game since Abbey had "beaten" her once again.

"Considering you're a kindergarten teacher and not a social worker, I think that counts as extra hours."

At that moment Paula, Abbey's mother pulled up in her rusty, dark green 2007 Honda Civic with a screech.

"I'm here!" she shouted as she quickly put her car into park and got out.

"Mommy!" Abbey said as she quickly hopped off the bench and onto her feet.

"Thank you again, Ms. Rivers," Paula said as she held the back door open for Abbey.

"You're welcome," Kylie said as she slowly stood to her feet.

"Mommy, I made you something in art today," Abbey said as she got in through the car door that Paula held open.

"That's good sweetie," Paula said as she buckled Abbey up in her seat belt.

"Paula, can I talk to you?" Kylie asked.

Paula shut the car door. "Uhm, sure."

"I don't mind watching Abbey after hours, she's a great girl and has a big heart. But I'm not a daycare center, I can't continue to keep her."

"I understand, this is the last time."

"You say that all the time Paula and then there's always another time. Is there not anybody she can stay with? Family members? Close friends?"

"Nobody, there's just me."

"How about a kid's center?"

"I can't afford it."

Kylie noticed the tears forming in Paula's eyes, she reached out and hugged her.

"It's ok, stop crying, things will get better. I will look into signing Abbey up for an after school program that will work with your hours.

You just keep your head up, be strong, and don't let your baby see you cry. I'll keep her until we figure something out."

"Thank you," Paula said as she dried her tears with her hands.

"You're welcome," Kylie said.

Kylie watched as Paula got into the car and she and Abbey drove off. She didn't know how she was going to help them out but she knew she had to for that little girl's sake.

"You have a way with people," Devin said as he sat on the bench,

Kylie turned around, as she had almost forgotten that he was there for a moment.

"I love what I do and I'd do anything to help out any of my kids. They're all my kids," Kylie said.

"The world needs more teachers like you."

She smiled as she sat down beside him. "What are you doing here?"

"I came to see you."

"Me?" she asked genuinely shocked.

"Yes you," he said with a slight chuckle.

"Why would you come here to see me?"

"Because I wanted to know if you wanted to go out to dinner with me."

She crossed her arms and raised an eyebrow at him. "You, Devin Jordan, want to have dinner with me?"

"Yes."

"Why?"

He chuckled and turned to face her. "Why are you questioning the fact that I want to go out with you?"

"Why do you want to go out with me? All the girls you come cross on a regular basis as a pro-baller, in this state alone. Just wondering why you choose to show up here and ask *me* out to dinner?"

"Yes," he said boldly.

"I don't understand."

"Why don't you just say yes? No need to make it make sense, just know that I chose you. That you are the only girl I'm wanting attention from in this moment."

She stared at him for a moment trying to figure out if he was being completely serious with her. His face didn't change so she knew that he was serious.

"Yeah I hear you," Kylie said as she shifted her wait on the bench.

There was a long pause before Devin responded by saying, "You didn't pass out when you first met me."

"And that's why you like me?"

He shrugged. "I guess."

"Well I guess you've got my attention now," she said, grinning at him flirtatiously at him.

*W*hy am I here again?" Camren asked Kylie as he sat in the dressing room area while she tried on dresses.

It was one of his rare days off and he was not enthused about spending it shopping. He watched as women walked in and out the store, praying that we would leave soon too.

"You're here to help me find a dress for my date tomorrow night."

"Could you hurry up? I don't want anybody to see me here," he said, looking around.

"How many times do I have to tell you not to rush a woman? It's rude."

"That's why I'm rushing you and not a woman."

"Ha, ha, ha, very funny. What do you think about this one?" she asked as she came out wearing a black dress that came just above her shins with a slit that reached her thigh.

"I like it," he said.

"But?"

"But is it appropriate? The slit is kind of high."

"Cam, you can't be serious, the slit is barely there."

"You don't want to be showing too much skin when you're going out with this dude."

She picked up her shoe and threw it at him. He ducked and it went over his head. He laughed as she went back into the dressing room.

"I hate you," she said.

"Love you too," he said.

"Y'all are so cute," the store clerk named Esther told Camren.

She had white hair and wrinkles, she wore her reading glasses on the bridge of her nose when she used them and around her neck on a pearl necklace when she wasn't.

"Thank you, but we're not a couple. She's too bossy for me," Camren said.

Kylie threw her other shoe and it hit him in his knee.

"Ouch!" he yelped as he rubbed his knee.

"Watch your mouth," Kylie said.

Esther laughed at them as she walked back over to the register.

"I feel bad for Devin."

"Oh hush, could you grab me another dress?"

"What's wrong with the black one?"

"The slit is too big," she said with mockery.

He huffed and then got up to grab another dress.

"I'm sorry but I couldn't help but overhear you and your girlfriend fussing over what dress to pick," a woman said to Camren as she walked up to the rack where he was.

She had blonde hair and a nice smile, the red lipstick she wore went nicely with the pumps she wore and the pants she wore fit her well. Her eyes were brown and her breasts were full.

"I'm not his girlfriend, he's not my type!" Kylie said.

"We're not together," Camren told the woman.

"Oh, well, I think I could help you guys out. What are we looking for?"

"A classy yet sexy dress that accentuates my body shape," Kylie said.

"What she said," Camren said.

The woman giggled. "I think this dress would be perfect."

She pulled out a glittery, red dress. She took it over to the dressing room that Kylie was in and handed it to her. Kylie tried it on and came out with a grin on her face.

"You look wonderful," the woman told Kylie. "I like it," Camren said. "But?" Kylie said. "No buts, Devin is going to love you in it."

"Great, we'll take it, he's paying," Kylie told the store clerk. Then she sauntered back into the dressing room.

Camren shook his head, then he introduced himself to the woman. "Camren."

"Hannah," she said giggling.

"Nice to meet you."

"Where are my shoes, Cam?" Kylie asked him.

"They're out here, come get them."

"Why can't you just throw them back, you know I'm overdue for a pedicure." "That's not my problem."

"That's exactly where we're going next and you're paying for that too."

"I don't think so."

Kylie gave Camren the dress to pay for, he walked over to the register and paid for the dress.

"Here you go, Dr. Blake," Esther said as she handed him back his visa card.

"Doctor, huh?" Hannah said as she peered around the rack at him.

"Orthopedic surgeon," he said as he put his card back into his wallet.

"That's nice, I actually broke my arm once when I was 12."

"I broke my arm as well, I was nine."

"What a fluke?"

"Right."

"Ready to go?" Kylie asked him.

"Yep, it was nice meeting you, Hannah," he said to her.

"Actually, I was wondering if you wanted to get drinks," Hannah said.

"Uh, I have to check my schedule-"

"But he's usually too busy," Kylie said.

Camren frowned at Kylie. "But I'd love to."

"Great, here's my number," Hannah said as she pulled her card out of her small purse and handed it to him.

"You're an insurance agent," Camren said as he read her card.

"Yes, my company is in the top ten in the state," Hannah said.

"Wow," he said.

"He'll be giving you a call," Kylie said. Then she dragged Camren out of the store.

♥ Camren had to deliver news to one of his patients about how the surgery hadn't gone according to plan. That was the part he hated most about being a surgeon, not able to provide great results for every person.

"I'm sorry, Ms. Fuller, but there's too much damaged tissue, we have to amputate your arm," Camren told his patient as he and the resident that was assigned to the case and also assisted with the surgery.

She began to cry, Camren excused himself from the room giving her time to think. He didn't want his emotions to get in the way of his professionalism, because what did he have to cry for.

"Hello, Dr. Blake," Bianca, one of the nurses said as she came up to him.

"Afternoon, nurse Williams," he said to her as he walked over to the desk and began writing on the chart in his hand.

"So I was wondering if you're free later tonight, I was thinking we could go get something to eat, maybe catch a movie," she said as she came up beside him and dragged her hand up and down his forearm.

"Um, I'll have to check my schedule and see if I have a surgery planned but I'll get back to you."

"See you later?" she said. Then she walked away.

"You are such a flirt," Kylie said as she walked up to Camren.

"I wasn't flirting," he said.

"You had the poor nurse hanging onto your every word."

A nurse came over the intercom calling for another doctor within the hospital to report to the emergency room. He handed the nurse behind the desk the chart and then turned to face Kylie.

"Not my fault," Camren said to Kylie.

74

She shook her head at him. "You're a flirt and don't even know you're a flirt."

"Whatever you say. What are you doing here anyways?" "Come to see April, she's being discharged today." "Oh that is right." "She's been asking about you."

"April?" he asked with raised eyebrows. She nodded. "Morgan just told her you'll be there." "Oh, really."

She raised an eyebrow at him. "Will you be there?"

He sighed. "I don't know."

"I've known you six almost seven years Camren and I've never seen you so afraid."

"I'm not afraid, I just don't want to go face Morgan's father again. He doesn't like me and I don't like him."

"But Kathy loves you and April's asking for you. Fight for what you want and go after it. Fight for the love of your life."

He dropped his head. "Morgan has a man in her life, she doesn't need me."

She touched his left cheek tenderly. "Camren, I see the love in your eyes. Your eyes sparkle whenever Morgan is in your sight."

That was another reason why he loved Kylie, she knew just what to say. She helped him get through medical school after he was so torn up over Morgan that he thought about quitting. Kylie let him know that he would be unhappy if he had, that if it was meant to be then they would find each other.

"Mr. Blake!" April exclaimed as Camren and Kylie entered her room.

"Hello, April," Camren said.

"What are you doing here?" Mike asked Camren kind of snarling at him.

"Just came to see her," Camren said.

"Hello, Camren," Kathy said to him.

"Hello, Mrs. Price," Camren said.

"Just call me Kathy, Kathy is just fine."

"Mrs. Price is what you say," Mike said, staring Camren down.

Camren stares right back at him, Kylie touched him on his shoulder.

"Camren? What are you doing here?" Morgan asked him as she entered the room with a chocolate pudding cup.

"Came to see April," he said, not taking his eyes off Mike.

"He was just leaving," Mike said.

"Stop it, Mike," Kathy said.

Mike grunted and crossed his arms. Camren was grateful for Kathy. Camren didn't understand why Mike had so much hate towards him. Ever since their first meeting Mike made it his mission to let Camren know that he didn't want him around.

"Surprised you came," Morgan said as she gave April the pudding.

"Just wanted to check up on April," Camren said, getting irritated.

"How's my favorite niece in the whole wide world?" Devin asked as he entered the room with balloons.

"Uncle DJ!" April shouted as she sat up.

"How you feeling, baby girl?"

She smiled. "Good."

"How about I take you to go get some doughnuts after you get outta here?"

"Cool!" she said as they fist bumped each other.

Devin sat the balloons down on the counter, and then spotted Kylie and walked over to her. He kissed her square on the lips, catching everyone in the room off guard. April was the only enthused one as she clapped and cheered.

"Hey," he said to her.

"Hi," she said with a huge smile.

"So I guess you two know each other," Camren said sarcastically as he gaped at them both.

"Yep, this is my new girl," Devin said proudly as he wrapped his arms around Kylie's waist.

"Girlfriend?" Camren said, looking over at Kylie.

She hadn't told him anything about seeing Devin, and that was their thing. They always shared things with each other, even things that aren't meant to be shared.

Her not telling Camren about Devin wasn't like her, she's usually bragging by now.

"Close your mouth, Cam," Kylie told him with a satisfied grin on her face. "Devin, you have not asked me to be your girlfriend yet, so it is not official."

"It's been on my mind, I thought after seven dates it would've made official," Devin said, smirking at her.

"I'm so happy for both of you," Kathy said.

"Thank you, Mrs. Price," Devin said.

"Thank you," Kylie said. "I thought we were going to wait until after the dinner."

"Sorry, I couldn't wait," Devin said with a shrug.

"Uncle DJ's gotta girlfriend!" April announced.

"That's right, Uncle DJ has a beautiful girlfriend," Devin said.

"Not until you ask me the question," Kylie hummed and wagged her finger.

"Well I'll get outta your hair," Camren said as he made his way to the door.

Morgan grabbed his hand before he could walk out the door. "Camren's gonna be joining us for dinner."

Mike gave them a mean look. If looks could kill Camren and Morgan would be dead. Camren wasn't sure if he was willing to sit at a dinner table and continue to be berated by her father.

"It would be wonderful to have you, dear," Kathy said, ignoring Mike.

"Thank you for sticking up for me, but I told you I can handle myself," Camren said to Morgan as she walked with him out of the room.

"He has to let things go, it's been years and he still has the same unknown grudge held against you," she said with a frown.

Camren shrugged. "That's just how your father is."

"He doesn't talk to Devin like that, what makes you so different."

"What about Tyler? He considers him to be his son in law. I actually haven't seen him since the party, doesn't he want to come see his daughter?"

"Uh, he's gonna meet us at the house," she stammered.

He stopped walking. "Maybe I shouldn't go to this dinner."

"Oh no you don't, I stood up for you now you're going," she said as walked over to him.

"If I go your father will have a fit."

"Good," she said with a roll of her neck.

"Morgan," he whined.

"Camren, you're going. Meet us at Sogo's at seven o'clock or you will have to deal with me," she threatened.

He cracked a smile. "I'll do my best."

"You better be there, doctor," she said as she walked back into the room.

Camren pulled up at the restaurant.

He had given himself several pep talks before arriving. He looked in the car mirror, gave himself one last talk, then took a deep breath and went inside. It was an Italian restaurant, the stone building was decorated in green vines, symbolizing their popular wine selections. The hostess showed him to the table and all eyes were on him.

"Glad you decided to join us again, I thought my husband had ran you off," Kathy said to Camren.

"Ah no ma'am, somebody who I find scarier than Mr. Price threatened me into coming," Camren said as he took a seat next to April.

It was Kylie who sat next to Devin, Mike sat next to Kathy who sat on the other side of April. Morgan sat on the other side of Camren and Tyler sat next to her.

"Where's your sister?" Camren asked Morgan.

"She went to a concert with some friends, said she'd been waiting a while for this day," Kathy said.

"And she would not have liked to have given up a Kehlani concert for a dinner," Morgan said.

Tyler, Devin and Mike struck up a conversation about sports. Camren's attention was drawn to April who was coloring. He noted that she was left-handed, as was he. That got him thinking about when she came to hospital and how worried Morgan got when she heard that a little girl was in the hospital. But the doctor had said the little girl was seven, Morgan told him that April was five, had she lied to him about her daughters' age? Why would she lie about that? How does lying about her age benefit in any way?

82

"Hey, April? What's your favorite color?" Camren asked her.

She continued coloring, but said, "My favorite color is green. People tell me that green is a boys color, but I disagree. And it matches my eyes"

"I agree, green is just a color and can be anybody's favorite color. My favorite color is yellow," Camren said.

"I like yellow, I have bows that I wear for all my softball games that are yellow. Because our jerseys are yellow and green."

"And how old are you?"

"I'm seven."

"What's with the third degree?" Mike growled at Camren.

Camren frowned, he felt Morgan tense up beside him. What was so wrong about him holding a conversation with April? It was harmless and he acted as if Camren was targeting his granddaughter.

"Just creating conversation, getting to know the child," Camren said in defense.

"Why? She doesn't need to know you, you're nobody to her," Mike said as Kathy tried grabbing him to calm him down.

"What's your problem with me? You've done nothing but cause issues with me" Camren said to Mike.

"Boy, don't start something you can't finish," Mike said as he stood up.

Camren stood up as well, he was ready for this to end. Morgan called his name, pulling at his arm. He then looked down at Morgan and saw her pleading for him to stay calm.

"Camren, please," she said, softly.

"Mr. Blake?" April said as she tugged on the back of his jacket.

He looked around at the table and saw everybody looking at him, took a deep breath and said, "Yes, April?"

"You're not supposed to yell in the restaurant," she whispered loudly.

Everybody at the table smiled, thankful for a moment of humor during that tense situation.

"Your right, April," Camren said. Then he looked at Morgan. "I'm gonna go." "Don't go, Camren," Kathy said.

"Please, stay," Kylie said. "No, I've already put some in a bad mood," he said as he pulled out his wallet. "Put that away, doc, we're paying," Devin told him.

"If that boy wants to pay, let him pay," Mike said, settling into his seat.

Kathy hit him on his chest and Morgan stared daggers into him.

"You be quiet, you've said enough," Kathy silenced Mike.

Camren kept his face as straight as possible like he did when he had to deliver bad news to his patients and their families. He then bid everybody a goodbye and then slowly walked away from the table and out the door.

♥ It had been three days since his outburst with Morgan's father at the restaurant. Camren couldn't believe he had let Mike get to him like that, he had never wanted that side of him to be shown but Mike pushed him there. Camren decided he wanted to give

Morgan a call to apologize for walking out on dinner that night.

"Camren?" Morgan said as she answered her phone.

"Hi," he said as he sat down on the beds in one of the on-call rooms.

He heard her walk from a noisy area to somewhere more quiet. "Everything alright?"

"Just called to apologize for the other night."

"For what?" she asked.

He could hear her messing around in the kitchen, he assumed she was making dinner.

"For arguing with your father at dinner, that was no way to act. We were there to celebrate Devin and Kylie and I made it about me."

"Who's that on the phone?" Tyler asked Morgan.

"One moment," she told him.

"I'm sorry if this is a bad time," Camren said.

He didn't want to admit it but hearing Tyler's voice in the background made him sort of jealous. But he knew that he was the man in her life so he had no choice but to respect it.

"Why do you do that?"

"Do what?"

She sighed. "You're so nice and considerate."
"Is that a bad thing or a good thing?" he asked as he laid down.

"It's aggravating. You're one of the most genuine and modest people I know."

"Maybe that's why your father disapproves of me."

She groaned. "My father feels threatened by you."

"Threatened? Why?"

She took a deep breath. "Because I was once so in love with you that I wanted to throw my career away."

"You we're?"

"Yes. couldn't you tell?"

That was music to his ears, he was glad to hear that he wasn't the only one that was so in love nothing else mattered. To disregard a life without her, a life that didn't have her in it was unimaginable.

"When did you meet April's father?"

He knew it was a bad move but it was too late to take it back. He needed answers because things weren't adding up. Was April his and Morgan was keeping it from him?

"Uh, after you."

"Y'all must've had a real love connection, y'all had a child for heaven's sakes."

"I guess. My mom is calling, can I call you back."

"I gotta go anyways, I'm on call."

It was partially true, but he wouldn't be needed that much tonight. He knew she was going to continue to avoid his questions until the truth just came out.

"Ok, bye."

"Bye." Then they hung up.

Camren laid there in bed staring up at the ceiling thinking about what his life would've been like if he had listened to his heart and not his brain. What if her father hadn't gotten in his head? What it would've been like to have kids with Morgan, to be married to her? Would be happier than he is right now? April had green eyes, Camren himself didn't have green eyes but his grandmother used to say when he was young he would have specks of green in his eyes. The more he thought about her the more he saw resemblance between him and April. He closed his eyes and decided to give his mind a rest.

♥ Morgan was riding in the back of the car with Devin thinking about Camren. He wouldn't tell her exactly where they were going but that she needed to ride with him. Ever since the night she and Devin showed up at the hospital and ran into Camren he's been on her mind. He always had her heart, no matter how many guys she dated none were ever anything like the love of her life. She did have his daughter after all. But she couldn't bring herself to tell him the truth though, she didn't want to lose him again.

"Something the matter?" Devin asked Morgan as he was texting.

"Not at all, why do you ask?"

"Because you have that worry line in your forehead," he said as he pointed at his own head for reference.

"There's no line and I'm not worried."

He placed his phone in his pocket and looked her in her eyes. "What's up?"

"It's nothing," she said with a sigh as she checked her email. "You've been acting weird ever since we saw the doc, what's up with you two?" "Camren is just an old college buddy." He raised an eyebrow. "He seems more like a college sweetheart." "What?"

"You know? One of the ones that got away, seems like it broke off before y'all could finish and now you're catching old feelings," he said as he took a drink from his water bottle.

"It was nothing," she said, looking out the window as they were stopped at a stop light. He gave her a look that said, 'really?'

"Ok maybe there was a little fling, but it was nothing, it's over with now."

He raised an eyebrow. "Doesn't seem like it's over, seems like there's some unfinished business."

"I'm telling you, DJ, there's nothing going on. The only thing we have in common is that we both want you to get better and get back out there onto the

Court."

He placed a gentle hand on her thigh. "Whatever you say." Then he pulled his phone back out.

"We never talked about how you injured your leg, I think it's time we discuss that."

"Don't worry about it, it was just an accident."

"I don't believe that."

He groaned. "I do, Morgan, so drop it."

She rolled her eyes. "You're mother called yesterday, she wants to see you. When's the last time you visited her?"

"Last thanksgiving."

"It's March, DJ," Morgan said with a frown.

He shrugged. "I've been busy."

"Well since we're here in your hometown, and you're recovering right now, how about we go visit?"

"No," he said in a stern voice.

"But it's your mother-"

"You know what, you're right. Driver, take me to my mother's house, it would be great to go home and see the old gang."

"It was just a suggestion, we don't have to."

"No, I'm glad you suggested it," he said with cynicism.

*T*hey pulled up at Devin's old home where he grew up, even though it had been years the place still brought back memories. The house was old, the paint had slowly chipped away and now the house had gone from forest green to a pale teal color and the red door was almost brown. The old rocking chair Devin used to fight his siblings over and sleep in his father's lap at night before being taken to bed, which he shared with his older brother. Devin and Morgan got out of the car and made their way into the small house.

"Ma!" Devin called out as he and Morgan entered the house.

There was no answer, Morgan took a look around the house. There were old family pictures of Devin and his brother and cousins on the walls and the long table by the door.

"Ma!" he shouted again.

"Who's nice car is in the yard, Bethany!" Devin's father, Frank, said as he came out of the bathroom and entered the room. He had a raspy voice, similar to Kenan Thompson's character in the movie Fat Albert.

"Pop," Devin said.

His father stopped in his tracks when he saw Devin, then he walked up to Devin and embraced him a big hug. Devin looked uncomfortable at first then he hugged his father back. The hug ended off with three hard pats to Devin's back.

"It's good to see you, my boy," Frank said as he let go of Devin.

Devin said, "Good to see you too, pop, where's ma?"

"She went to the store, she should be back any minute, this your girl? She's a pretty one." "No, this is my agent, Morgan." Frank held out his hand to Morgan. "Agent? Sounds like a pretty powerful woman."

"Agent slash assistant. I'd like to think of myself as such though. Holding the key to your son's future in sports," Morgan said with a slight chuckle as she shook his hand.

"Well I'll make sure to have my wife to make you her famous apple pie."

"Frank, who's nice car is in the yard," Devin's mother, Bethany, said as she came in the house carrying a brown paper bag full of groceries.

"That would be mine," Devin said.

Her jaw dropped and she kind of tossed the bag onto the table, then she ran to Devin and hugged him tight.

"Hey, momma," he said as he hugged her back.

"It's been a minute, son, it's good to see you," she said as she pulled back and placed her hands on either side of his face.

"Good to see you, momma," he said, grinning.

"Who's this?"

"This is Morgan."

"She's pretty," she said, but the word 'pretty' sounded more like 'purtty.'

"That's what I said, he said she's not his girlfriend," Frank said.

"Too bad," Bethany said with a shrug.

"Thank you," Morgan said, smiling from ear to ear.

"Where do you want me to put these other bags?" Devin's brother, Raymond, asked as he entered through the screen door.

"On the table. Ray, your brother came to visit us," said Bethany.

"Well, well, well, if it isn't the superstar himself," Raymond said as he sat the bag of groceries down on the table with the others.

Morgan looked between Devin and Raymond and saw the uneasy tension, there seemed like there was something built up from years back.

"What an honor it is to have you amongst our presence," Raymond said dramatically.

"Oh stop it, Ray," said Frank. "Bethany, why don't you make our guest one of your famous apple pies."

"Of course I will, you two staying for dinner?" asked Bethany.

"No, I have some business to attend to," Devin said.

"Oh okay. What happened to your leg son? We heard about it on the internet but we know better than to believe everything that's posted on the internet," said Frank.

Devin looked at Raymond and Raymond glared back at Devin with a smug look on his face.

"I was playing ball with some guys and I came down the wrong way," said Devin.

Raymond glared at Devin, Morgan didn't know what was going on but she knew that there was an untold story.

"We have to get going, just wanted to come by to see you guys," Devin said.

"No, stay for dinner," Bethany whined.

"We have to be somewhere, right Morgan?" Devin asked her.

"Uh, right," she stuttered.

"Oh ok, another time?" asked Frank.

"I'll be back to see you soon, pop," Devin said as he and his father hugged.

"I'll hold you to that."

"It was nice meeting you all," Morgan said as she and Devin made their way out of the house.

"Devin," Morgan said after riding in the car in uncomfortable silence for more than 30 minutes.

"Yes, Morgan?" he said, sounding irritated.

"What was that?"

"What was what?"

"We go over to your parents' house and the guy who tried to break your leg walks into the house."

"He's my brother, Morgan."

"Excuse me?"

"His name is Raymond Jordan, he's my older brother."

♥ Saturday morning Camren was jogging through town, he came to a stop when he saw Morgan and April go inside an ice cream parlor. He thought it was a complete coincidence to run into them. He decided to go in after them.

"Hi, Mr. Blake," April said when she spotted him.

"Hello, April," he said to her.

"You getting ice cream too?"

He smiled and nodded. "Yes I am."

"Good, you can sit with us," she said as she grabbed his hand.

Morgan smiled at them, they all gave their orders to the woman working. Then they found a booth, Morgan gave Camren her ice cream to hold while she took a call.

"What flavor did you getting, Mr. Blake?" April asked Camren as they sat in the booth.

"Birthday cake," he said.

"I like birthday cake but rainbow is my favorite," she said as she licked her ice cream cone.

"Ah, you look like a rainbow type of girl."

"Really?"

"Uh-huh."

"What about mommy? What flavor type is she?"

"Hmm," he said, pretending to think. "She looks like a pecan girl."

"She is, wow, you're good," she said, nodding,

He chuckled before he ate a spoonful of ice cream. "It's from years of experience."

"I play softball, my team is really good," she said as she licked some of her ice cream. "Do you like softball?"

"I do."

"I play center field and pitcher. Mommy used to be a left fielder."

"Are you as good as your mommy?"

She shrugged and she licked at her ice cream. "I don't know."

"What are you guys talking about?" Morgan asked as she returned to the booth.

"Softball," April said.

Camren handed Morgan her cup of pecan ice cream. "I didn't know you played softball."

"It was just a hobby."

"Grammie has all her trophies in a case," April said.

"Sounds like you were a star," he said to Morgan.

She shook her head. "No, April's the star. She has the best arm on the team, her fastball is dangerous."

"It's alright, mom," April whined.

"No, not just alright, you should see it, Cam," Morgan said.

"Maybe you could come to my next game," April said.

Camren chuckled at the sight of April, she had ice cream all on her lips and a little on her cheek. Camren reached over with a napkin and wiped her face for her, she smiled and thanked him.

"The doctor cleared you?" he asked her.

Morgan ate a spoonful of ice cream. "She goes in for a checkup Monday."

"I would love to come see you play," Camren said to April.

"Great," April said with excitement. Then she dug into her ice cream cone.

Camren hopped on a plane to

Denver to go see April play. He didn't know what he was doing, going to the softball game of a little girl who potentially could be his. It was something about April that made him feel something, he had a soft spot for her. The flight wasn't too bad, he just preferred not to fly. He followed the directions that Morgan gave him and showed up to the game a few minutes early. All the players weren't there yet, but April was there. She was practicing her pitch with the coach, Camren assumed. Camren saw Morgan sitting with the other moms in the bleachers, he just stood by the fence and watched.

"So you just show up and don't speak?" Morgan asked as she snuck up beside him.

"It wasn't intended to hurt your feelings," he said, smiling.

"I think I'll survive," she said.

They watched April throw a strong curveball. April seemed to be a natural athlete and real passionate about the game. Her French braid whipped around as she moved, she kept a serious expression as she threw.

"She's pretty good," he said.

"Learned from the best."

"Let me guess, you?"

"The one and only."

They laughed together. Then two of the other team member's mothers came over to them.

"Hey, Morgan. Who's this gentleman?" Sarah, a woman with brown hair in a tight ponytail and T-shirt that said I'm a mom of three.

"Hello, Sarah, this is Camren, Camren, this is Sarah and Tony," Morgan introduced them.

"Hi," he said as he waved at them both.

"You have eyes just like April's," Tony, the woman standing beside Sarah, said.

She had long brown hair that she wore in loose curls around her shoulders, she had three earring holes in her left ear and two in her right. It was funny to hear yet another person to point to similar features between him and April.

"He does," Sarah chimed in.

"Lucky coincidence," Morgan said with a nervous laugh.

"Yes but anyways, we came over to ask you if April is bringing snacks for next week's game?"

"Oh yes, she will."

"Great, don't forget Samantha is allergic to peanuts," Tony said as they walked away.

"We have the same eyes?" Camren asked Morgan as he watched the team warm up.

"Yours is a darker green," she said as she leaned against the fence.

"You know you don't have to stand here beside me, right?"

"Will it bother you if I do?"

He just shook his head. She stood beside him for every inning, he wanted to tell her to go sit in the bleachers but he was enjoying her company too much. He would watch as she nervously racked her fingers through her hair when the score got close or when April was up to bat. Some things never changed, those were the same nervous habits she had back then. After the game was over and April's team had won 7 to 3, April and her friend, Isabella, came over to Morgan and Camren.

"You came!" Morgan said to Camren.

"I told you I would," he said.

"This your dad?" the little girl standing beside April asked.

Camren's eyebrows raised at the question, it was the same one running through his mind as well. The little next to April had teeth missing everywhere, a few were trying to grow back in. She had big brown eyes and her jersey was dirty from sliding onto the plates.

"No, this is my mom's friend. He's a doctor," April told her.

"Oh ok, I'm Isabella," the girl told Camren.

"Nice to meet you," he told her.

"Mom, can Izzy stay over?" April asked Morgan.

"We were supposed to do that thing today," Morgan said to April.

"We'll do it tomorrow, please, mom," April begged.

"Is this ok with your dad, Isabella?" Morgan asked.

"Yes ma'am," Isabella said.

"And I have clothes for her to wear, so she doesn't have to worry about packing a bag," April said.

"Well alright," Morgan said with slight hesitance.

"Thank you," April said as she and Isabella walked away.

"Girls will be girls," Camren said. "Well I enjoyed the game-"

"Where do you think you're going?" she asked him.

"Back to my hotel," he said with a raised eyebrow.

"Oh no you don't, you are not leaving me with two hyper-active girls by myself all day," she said.

"What about Tyler?"

"He has business to take care of," she said, sounding kind of disappointed.

Camren shrugged. "I guess I can spare a few hours to help out an old friend of mine."

She playfully slapped his arm. "Don't you ever put old and me in the same sentence."

They both laughed, then April and her friend joined them carrying their softball bags on their backs.

Camren made the suggestion for them to go to the fair, Morgan was accepting of it because it meant she didn't have to cook tonight or worry about entertaining the girls. And the girls were ecstatic, all they heard was rides and sweets. They arrived at the fair later that evening, the first thing April and Isabella wanted to get on the merry-go-round. Then it was funnel cakes and turkey legs, followed by all the rides within the fair.

"You're spoiling her you know?" Morgan said to him as they stood outside the gate as April and Isabella rode on the ride.

"How so?" he asked.

"By buying her ice cream and bringing her to the fair and buying her a stuffed animal."

"Just being friendly."

"Well I thank you anyways." Then she looped her arm through his.

He looked down at their conjoined arms, then at her. She beamed at him and he held her arm back. She looked as beautiful now as she did on their first date.

"Mommy!" April yelled from the ride.

Morgan waved at them with her free arm as they passed by. This whole situation was odd to him, him linking arms with her as her daughter rode on a ride It looked as if they were a couple, even though she already has a man in her life.

"Camren Blake, is that you?" Heather, a woman Camren used to see a couple months back, asked from behind them.

Camren rotated around with his arm still looped with Morgan's to see Heather standing there with her too high heels and her skin tight dress. Her brown hair was down and her make-up was on. He knew this wouldn't be a good interaction.

"Hello, Heather," he said to her.

"New fling I see," she said, looking Morgan up and down frowning.

He shrugged. "Something like that."

"I can tell you now that he's a very selfish lover," she told Morgan.

Morgan just grinned at Heather like her words weren't affecting her. "Oh he is, is he?"

Camren saw the devilish look in her eyes, despite her friendly smile on her face. He had experienced one too many times in high school, he knew that meant that she was ready to silently strike at any given moment. He didn't need to be told twice, he recognized when to step back and let her do her thing.

"Yes, it's all about him," Heather said, rolling her neck.

"Tell me about it, these men. Thank you for warning me."

"Uh-huh, let's see how long this one lasts. He's also afraid of commitment," Heather said, looking Camren up and down.

"Mommy, look at the doggy. Can we get a puppy?" April asked Morgan, pointing at a small, gray pit-bull as she and Isabella came over after the ride was over.

"Maybe someday, baby," Morgan told April.

"Ok," April said with disappointment.

"So you got a baby with her?" Heather asked Camren.

"Oh yeah, and that hand thing that he does," Morgan whispered to Heather. "He learned that from me"

Morgan winked at Heather, Heather looked at Camren. He just shrugged. Her nostrils flared, she gave them both dirty looks and then walked away with a huff.

"Who was that lady? She wore too much makeup," Isabella said with a scrunched nose.

"One of your patients?" Morgan asked Camren.

"Yeah, I was there when she got her girls enlarged," he said.

They both laughed. Then they and the girls continued walking around looking for the next thing that would catch the girls' attention.

"What's your favorite color, Mr. Blake?" Isabella asked Camren as they walked around.

"Orange," he said.

"Mines is Pink," Isabella said.

"Mines too!" April said. "I have a dress that matches one of my baby doll's dresses."

They squealed and hugged. He smiled at them and then looked over at Morgan, who was smiling as well.

"Mr. Blake, do you know mommy's favorite color?" April asked.

"Purple," he said.

"Do you know why?"

"Her first stuffed animal was purple, she got him when she was about your age."

"She said his name was Mr. Winkie," April said.

"Be quiet, April," Morgan said with embarrassment.

"Oh really?" Camren asked as he laughed.

"Mhmmm, she still has this one stuffed animal she got from my daddy."

Morgan froze and her face looked panicked. "April!"

"What's the animal look like?" asked Isabella.

"It's a blue and yellow giraffe, his name's Lucas."

Camren gave Morgan a giraffe on their second date. It couldn't be the same giraffe. Morgan looked over at Camren, a look of worry flashed in her eyes.

"That was very nice of your daddy, wasn't it?" Camren asked April.

"Yes it was," April said. "I can barely get my boyfriend to get me a pudding at lunch."

"Boyfriend?" said Morgan.

"Yeah, she dates Jacob Young. He plays soccer," Isabella said.

"What do you say y'all get on this ride?" Camren asked as he pointed to a small purple roller coaster, trying to come to their rescue.

"Yes!" April and Isabella said at the same time.

"I can't believe she said she has a boyfriend," Morgan said.

"Calm down," Camren said with a chuckle.

He wasn't going to bring up the fact that April had brought up a question he had been asking himself but was avoiding. That he possibly could be the father of Morgan's child, that he just might be a dad. He pondered that thought as he watched April and Isabella.

"Thank you for today," Morgan told Camren as he carried both Morgan and Isabella in each arm up the stairs of her condo to April's room.

*T*hey had fallen asleep on the way home and Morgan didn't want to wake them so Camren offered to carry them inside. Each of their heads laid peacefully on his shoulders.

"You're welcome," he said.

He laid them both on the bed, Morgan came in behind him and started removing their shoes and tucked them under the Princess and the Frog themed cover.

"I enjoyed myself tonight," he told Morgan as they left April's room.

"It's nice spending time with April before I have to get back to working again," she said, closing the door.

"What do you mean?"

"Yeah, Devin's been working on his leg and he's going to get back out there and play in the next game," she said as they made their way back down the stairs of the condo.

"Well, if that's what he wants to do." "I don't see how he's gonna play when he can barely walk on it. The coach is gonna check him out and see if he's ready." "I wouldn't play just yet if I were him."

"Would you care for a cup of coffee?" she asked as they walked through her kitchen. "I've already had enough coffee for today." "One more cup wouldn't hurt." "Sure." Then he took a seat on the bar stool at her marble island.

"Just because it's what he wants doesn't mean it's what's best," he said.

"That's true, I've tried to advise him against the idea. That I would talk the team into waiting for him until he's all healed up."

"But at the end of the day it's his decision."

She grabbed the coffee grounds and two mugs out of the cupboard. "That's true, but it's still not fair. He's not just messing with his career, he's also putting mine on the line too."

Camren didn't respond, he was trying to get his thoughts together so he could say the right thing.

"Nice place you have here," he finally said.

"Thanks, nice place to rent out while we're here," she said as she poured the coffee beans and water into the coffee maker.

"Still looks nice in here."

"Does your place look anything like this?"

"What? Clean?"

She giggled. "No, I mean does it still look like your college dorm room?"

"Oh no, not at all. I mean there's some clothes on the floor, but it's more like a bachelor's pad."

"Ah, I see, it's empty," she said with a nod as she turned the machine on.

He chuckled. "So how's life been treating you these past few years?"

She came over and sat with him. "Good I guess, wasn't easy at first raising a kid on my own."

"Bet it's hard to explain to her his absence."

"Yeah, it is."

The silence picked up, it lasted until the coffee maker stopped. She got up and went to make their cups.

"Cream or sugar?" she asked him remotely.

"Both."

She nodded and made their coffees.

"I'm sorry," he said randomly.

"What are you apologizing for now?" she asked as she poured coffee into the mugs.

"For hurting you, for making you feel some type of way about me, about us. I was stupid but I never intended to hurt you."

"Camren, that was seven years ago, we've grown since then," She brought the mugs of coffee over to the table. "I have a six-year-old to raise and focusing on the past will only disrupt things."

"I understand."

He sipped his coffee, they sat there for a moment. They each wanted to say something but didn't know what to say or how to say it. "Well it's getting late, I better go," Camren said as he stood up.

"Ok," she said, not really wanting him to go just yet.

"You have a goodnight, Morgan."

"Camren."

"Yeah?" he said as he stopped his movements.

"That day you invited me to your dorm room so you can tell me that you wanted to break up with me, I thought I saw a look of regret in your eyes. I don't think you really wanted to break up with me."

He wanted to tell her the truth, that he wanted nothing more than to confess to her all the secrets she was unaware of.

"The only regret I had was not being able to keep you from crying."

"So that day you were really done with me? You really wanted to see other people? Was I not good enough?"

"It wasn't like that, Morgan."

"Please explain it to me, Cam, because I wanna know. Was it because I wasn't like those other girls that panted over you? Was it because I wasn't as pretty as Joslin Mendez?"

"Oh come on, Morgan, you know I never had any interest in Joslin."

"How come she was dancing all over you at a frat party?"

"It was a party, people dance, but she wasn't dancing with me."

"My friend Tracy saw y'all."

"Your friend Tracy was one of those girls that wanted me."

She huffed. "You know what? Forget I ever asked."

She got up and moved around the counter. He stood up from his chair and went over to her.

"Morgan, listen to me, I never loved someone the way I loved you. I searched all over but I couldn't find it. You were a great girlfriend and I don't want you to think otherwise, I just made a mistake and you just happened to have gotten hurt. I don't want anything more than for you to be happy."

"I wasn't happy for the six months after our breakup, all I did was cry and eat. It might have been the pregnancy hormones and cravings but I still felt miserable. Then April was born and I fell in love with this tiny human, I looked into her eyes and I saw you. I saw the man that I once loved, that I'm still in love with."

He all of a sudden felt the need to grab a hold of her and kiss her. He reached out, grabbed her and pulled her in close.

"What are you doing?" she asked.

He didn't respond, he gripped the back of her neck and brought her mouth to his. She stood there first but then she wrapped her arms around his neck and kissed him back. He pulled her in tighter, he had been dreaming about this moment for far too long. He backed her up against the fridge and squeezed her round ass. She whimpered and a breathy moan escaped from her body, then she pulled away.

"Oh my god, Camren," she said as her hands went to her mouth.

"I don't know what to say."

"You should go."

"Yeah," he said as he started towards the door. Then he left the condo, he went home that night and beat himself up.

Camren was out on a dinner

date with Hannah, he had called her a couple days after he got back from Denver. Actually Kylie took his phone and messaged her forcing him to have to call and explain. They talked for half an hour or so and then made plans for dinner. He had to admit that when he had seen her in her red blouse that hung just slightly off her left shoulder. She had her beach curls behind her ear putting her pearl earrings on display.

"I was glad you could make it to dinner," she said as she sipped on her red wine.

They had just finished their dinner, they had both gotten the spaghetti. They were just about to order dessert.

"Same here, it seems every time I get a moment to myself I get called in," he said.

"Shouldn't say that too loudly, Dr. Blake, you might jinx yourself."

He chuckled. "Not too worried."

"Must be exciting working with people and bones all the time."

"I enjoy what I do, not being able to save every life is the worst part."

"You have a brain and a heart, I like that in a man," she said with a smile.

He smiled too. "You seem to have a brain as well, Ms. Insurance Agent."

"Brain and beauty is a great combo as well."

"Yes it is," he said with a nod.

"Tell me, how's your insurance."

"Is this the part where you talk me into switching companies?"

She chortled. "Not at all, this is the part where I try to use big words to make myself feel better and to make you think I'm smarter than I look."

They just sat there smiling at each other. That's when he saw Kylie come running into the restaurant, she looked hysterical.

"Kyles, what's the matter?" he asked as he stood up and met her halfway.

"We have to go, it's Devin. He overplayed his knee and they had to rush him to the hospital."

"I'm so sorry, Hannah, can we do this another time?" he asked her.

"Of course, you go ahead," she said.

"Thank you," he pulled out his wallet.

He paid for the dinner and then left out with Kylie. They hopped on the next plane to Denver,

Morgan texted him the address to Sky Ridge Medical Center. When they showed up Morgan and some of Devin's teammates were in the lobby waiting.

"What's his update?" Camren asked Morgan.

"He won't let anybody touch him, all they can do is give him pain meds. He wants to see you," she told him.

He asked the front desk nurse about Devin, he then walked into the room to hear Devin fussing at the Orthopedic surgeon, Peyton Strong.

Her blonde hair was shiny, her teeth were sparkling and her eyes were a deep blue. She reminded him of a young Merideth Gray.

"Camren Blake, Orthopedic surgeon at St Vincent Carmel Hospital," Camren said to her.

"Dr. Blake, please tell this woman that I do not need surgery," Devin said to Camren.

Camren and Devin shared a brief glance.

"You gonna tell her or should I?" Camren asked Devin.

"I don't want the surgery," Devin said with a sigh.

"You need to have the surgery, any added pressure to your previously torn muscle will damage your chances of ever using your knee again," Peyton told him.

"How do I know that this surgery won't make my knee any worse than it already is. My boy came and got work done on his foot, now he can never play football again," Devin said.

"I'm pretty sure Dr. Strong knows what she's doing," Camren said.

Devin just shook his head. He was very stubborn, Camren commended him on sticking to his guns. But Camren also knew that playing ball was real important to Devin

"You want to continue to play basketball then this is your best option, get this surgery and we'll go from there. And I know if you love basketball just as much as I love being a doctor then he would do whatever it takes."

Devin hesitated. "Give me your word?"

"I give you my word that you're in good hands. We'll do the best we can to help you."

"I will only get this surgery if you do it."

Camren turned and looked at the other doctor, she shrugged and nodded.

"I'll join in on the surgery but doctor Strong will be taking the lead."

"Ok," Devin said with a sigh.

"You'll go back to playing again by the start of the next season," Peyton assured him

"How is he? Is he alright?" Kylie asked Camren as he came out to inform them on Devin's situation.

She, Morgan and a handful of his teammates were in the waiting area. The surgery was very successful, he had to give his props to doctor Strong. She was amazing in the operating room, if she wasn't located so far away he would think they would make a great team.

"He's unconscious at the moment, we used a graft to replace the ligament and he should recover in the next six to nine weeks," he told her.

She hugged him tight. "Thank you."

"You're welcome."

"When can we see him?" Morgan asked.

"When they transfer him to the ICU," he said.

Tyler came over to comfort Morgan. Camren found it odd that he was here since he had seen him around in weeks. If he was here what did the kiss mean?

"When's the last time y'all spoke?" Kylie whispered to Camren.

"About a week ago," he said.

"That's sad," she said, frowning up at him.

"We both have our own lives to live."

"Too busy living to pick up the phone and text or call?" He nodded. "I *am* a doctor, Kylie." "And I'm a school teacher and she's a sports agent, so what?" He shrugged. "It's just not gonna work out, I have my job and she has her life and a kid to focus on."

"But where's the love?"

He shrugged and then walked away to go check on Devin. He didn't know what the next step was when it came to him and Morgan. He didn't even know where they stood now that was one amongst many questions he needed to ask her.

♥ Everybody was gathered at the hospital in Devin's room, everybody except his parents. Even Kathy also made it to see him, Camren wasn't sad to say that he was glad that her husband didn't make an appearance. He was not wanting to exchange the routine blows.

"Would you prefer a live band or a DJ for our wedding?" Devin asked Kylie as he sat up in his bed.

"Wedding?" Camren said to Kylie.

"I don't remember you popping the question," Kylie said to Devin.

"Not yet, but I will eventually," he said.

"Are you sure about that? We've only known each other a couple weeks"

"And I feel closer to you than any woman in my life."

"I haven't even met your family yet, I mean why aren't they here?"

He paused, his face turned stern. "If meeting my parents is what it'll take to then I'll make an arrangement for you to see them."

"You're serious?" she asked with wide eyes.

"I am. Morgan, call Jenny and tell her to call my mother and set up a dinner date," he told Morgan. "And also tell her I'm in the hospital but not to worry."

She nodded. "I'll get right on it when we leave here," Morgan said.

"I want a live band," Kylie said, grinning.

"Sounds good to me. Any in particular?" he asked.

"1991," Camren and Kylie said at the same time.

They had just shared an inside joke, Devin and Morgan looked at them like they were crazy.

"I feel like I've missed out on something," Devin said as he sat up in his hospital bed.

"That makes two of us," Morgan said as she handed April a tablet to play on. "I'll tell you later," Kylie told Devin.

They discussed a band and what music would be planned for a hypothetical wedding that was not yet planned. To hear Kylie discussing her future with a guy who she obviously was crazy about was music to Camren's ears. He couldn't help but smile from ear to ear at their blossoming love.

"Momma, can we go to the cafeteria?" April asked as she got up from her chair. "You had a snack, April," Morgan said.

"I'll take her down to the cafeteria right quick," Camren told Morgan.

"If you're sure," she said with uncertainty.

"Let's go, April," he said to her as he gave her his hand to hold.

She grabbed it and he led them to the cafeteria.

"So what do you want, April? Want some chips, maybe a muffin, cookies?" he asked as they stood in the cafeteria.

"Mommy doesn't allow sweets during the day, so I'll take a muffin. I only eat the banana nut kind though," she said.

He chuckled, she reminded him of her mother. "Alright, banana nut muffin it is then."

"Your daughter is so adorable, she has your eyes," a woman said as she passed by them.

She had blue eyes and she wore pink scrubs and a white coat. He looked at April and he saw that she was right, she did have some of his facial features.

"What's your dad like, April?" he asked her as they made their way back to Devin's room.

"I don't know, mommy says he's smart and handsome. I don't think he's so smart," she said as she ate one of her cookies.

"Why do you say that?" "If he was smart he wouldn't have left us," she said sadly. "Maybe he thought he was doing what was best for you and your mommy." "Or maybe he didn't want me," she said with a sad face.

He stopped and got down on her level. "I assure you it had nothing to do with you, you're a bright and friendly little girl."

"I guess."

"How do you feel about Mr. Tyler?"

"He's alright, he's too boring and I know mommy doesn't really like him."

"Oh really?" "Yea, she thinks he's boring too. Maybe you can be my daddy." He chuckled. "I don't know about that."

"Mommy won't mind, she likes you. We could go to the fair again!"

He handed her the muffin to hold as they stood in line at the register. "She just might mind."

"Will you come to my next softball game?"

"Sure, if I don't have a patient. Just tell your mommy to let me know what day." "Ok," she said as she nodded with enthusiasm.

Camren was helping his

grandparents clean out their attic. His grandmother was wanting to make more room and his grandfather was wanting to have a mancave. They were still "discussing it", he knew his grandmother would win in the end. His grandmother was upstairs dusting so he thought this would be a good time to call Morgan about April's game.

"Hello," she said, answering the phone.

He took a deep breath, hearing her voice still caught his breath. "Uh hey, sorry if I'm interrupting anything. I'm just calling because April and I had a conversation about her next softball game, she gave me the invitation and told me to get with her assistant about the date and time."

She chuckled. "I swear that girl is something else." "Strong minded, reminds me of a certain somebody." "Her game is at 2:30 this Saturday. They play their biggest competitor. April can't stop talking about it."

"Ah sounds like a game I can't miss."

"Great."

"Hey, Morgan?" "Yea?"

He moved closer to the window to enjoy the view as he talked. "Are you busy right now?" "Not at the moment, why?"

"I just want to talk to you."

There was silence on her end for a minute or two. "Ok."

Before he could get into the question on whether or not April was his, or ask about her future plans after Devin heals and whether or not they included him, or even clarify what happened between them in her kitchen. He heard a male voice in the background.

"Who's that on the phone?" Mike's voice boomed from the other end of the phone. "A friend," she said.

"What's their name?"

"It's Camren, he wanted to know when April's game is."

"He can't come." "I'll call you back, Cam," she said.

But she didn't hang up and he wasn't sure if he was supposed to hang up since she didn't, but then he heard their conversation.

"What's the big deal, daddy?," Morgan asked him.

"I don't want that son of a-"

"Daddy!"

"He's no good for you, baby, I don't want him around April!" he shouted.

"Well, daddy, you have no say."

"I have no say?"

"He's her father."

Camren felt like he had been slapped. He was a father, he was April's father. His suspicions were correct but he didn't think it was actually true. Him? A father?

"You said her father had died," Mike said.

131

"When we broke up it felt like he had disappeared from my life forever, now that he's back maybe I should let him father his child."

Camren could hear things clattering, her growing more anxious for what else could be revealed to him. "I am fairly disappointed in you, getting knocked up by some hoodlum."

"He is not some hoodlum, he has morphed into a great man. A man that you could-"

"Oh spare me, Morgan, call me when you get some sense."

Camren hung up the phone, his jaw was on the floor. How come she didn't tell him sooner? Why didn't he put things together? The little girl's age, Morgan's avoidance. He just wasn't ready to hear this, he wasn't prepared for the news that he's a father. A father of a six-year-old little girl.

"You ok, sweetheart?" Camren's grandmother asked him as she walked down the stairs.

"Oh, uh, yeah. Just thinking about work," I said as I absent-mindedly went through the box of books.

"You sure? Frown any harder and you'll create lines."

"Yeah I'm fine," he said. Then he cleared his throat. "Think I'ma go get a Pepsi from the fridge. You want one grams?"

"No thank you I have tea brewing," she said as she looked through another box he had brought down earlier. She grabbed an old photo album. "Awe, my how I miss you being this little."

He walked over to take a look at the photos. "Ah, wasn't I handsome?"

"Yes, had your father's cheek bone structure," she said, squeezing his cheek.

"I miss them," he said with sorrow.

"I know, sweetie, me too," she said, flipping through.

She stopped at a picture of Camren with arms wrapped around each of his parent's necks, with him only wearing a black wife-beater and blue briefs. He couldn't have been more than six in the picture.

That's when he realized he wanted moments like this with April and Morgan.

He wanted to share moments like her hoping on her bike and riding it around the neighbor and he would shout, "Don't get a ticket!" because she was pedaling too fast.

He wanted to have awkward talks about life like he had with his mom. A tear slipped from his eye, he was so sad that a car accident had taken away the most important people in his life

"Cam, would you stop pacing and tell me what's going on?" Kylie asked as they stood in the living room of her apartment.

He had called as soon as he had left his grandparents' house. He had to let her know what he had found out. He had gone straight to her house without notice so she had let him have it for interrupting a night that was on the path to a happy ending including Devin.

"I can't believe this," he said as he continued to pace back and forth in her kitchen.

"Camren, you're leaving a dent in my carpet," she said as she sat at her table snacking on cheese and crackers.

"I'm a father, Kylie."

She stood up from her coach. "Wait, what?"

"I'm the father of Morgan's daughter, April is mines."

"Camren, are you serious?"

"Yes, I overheard Morgan and her father having a discussion about me and it just popped up."

"Oh my god, Cam, you're a father."

"I know," he said as he started pacing harder.

"Alright, alright, Cam, sit down," she said as she grabbed him by his shoulders and lowered him down in a car beside hers.

"I'm a father, Kyles," he said, completely befuddled.

"So April is your daughter?"

"She has my eyes and my smile. She does that thing with her ear when she's sleepy that I used to do when I was younger."

"So I see you're taking this pretty good."

"Yeah, I mean I'm almost 30 and I'm only getting older. Why not have a child? Why not get involved in the life of the daughter I never knew was mine?"

"Wow," she said in genuine shock.

"I mean think about it, Kyles."

"I'm glad you feel this way, now tell Morgan."

My whole mood changed. "How do I do that?"

"Just come out with it, let her know that being in your daughter's life is what you want to do. That you want to be there when April grows up."

"I've already missed out on six years."

"At least it wasn't her whole life."

♥ Hey, Morgan, an emergency surgery came up. I can't make it to April's game. Tell her I'm sorry and let me know when her next scheduled game so I can make it to that one," Camren said as he left a message on Morgan's phone right before he went into surgery to repair a broken femur.

"Dr. Blake, it's time," one of the nurses told me.

He hung up the phone and then went to start the surgery and went to save a life. "The surgery went well, I treated the broken femur with plates and screws and your son should be able to use this leg in the next four to six months," Camren told the parents of the young boy.

"Thank you so much, Dr. Blake," the mother said as she hugged him.

"You're welcome," he said with a smile as he hugged her back.

"I appreciate it, doc," the father said.

"It's what I do every day," Camren said as he shook his hand.

When he was done talking to the family he checked his phone and found a voicemail from Morgan, he went into a janitor's closet to listen to it.

"Hey, Camren, I was calling to tell you that April and her team won. April had two home-runs and pitched a great game. She was kind of disappointed that you weren't here but I explained to her that you would try to make it to the next one. I also wanted to talk to you face to face about something really important. Call me when you get a chance."

He was about to call her back when the door opened and then closed. He looked up to see nurse Courtney leaning against the door.

"Hey there, sexy," she said as she advanced towards him.

"Um, nurse Beatty," he said.

"Yes, What do you need, doctor? I can give anything you need."

"I need to take a personal call."

She smiled seductively. "Call to your girlfriend, sounds exciting. I promise to be quiet."

"Please, Courtney."

"Begging, that's sexy," she said, giggling.

Just then someone opened the door, Courtney quickly moved away from him. "Sorry," one of the other nurses said as she quickly closed the door back.

Camren made his exit, dialing up Morgan's number. She picked up quickly, so quick he didn't get a chance to get his wording together.

"Uh, I'm sorry to be calling so late, but you said you had something important to talk to me about" Camren said.

"Yes, it's something really important and I think we should discuss this face to face."

"I really wish we could but the ER is swamped and so am I."

"You really need to hear this."

"Alright, come to the hospital."

He was already in the ER working on in-coming patients when Morgan arrived. He excused himself and then pulled her into one of the private rooms.

"I only have a couple of minutes, so we have to make this quick," he told her.

"Tell me, Camren," she said as she walked around the room.

"Tell you what?"

"Tell me why you really broke up with me all those years back?"

"This is what we're gonna discuss?"

She crossed her arms and gave him a look.

"Like I told you then, I-"

"It just wasn't working for you, I remember those exact words coming out of your mouth but to this day I still don't believe you."

"What do you want me to say?"

"I want you to tell me the truth."

"You want the truth? You want me to tell you the real reason why I broke things off?"

She nodded. "Yes."

"Your father, he told me that his princess deserved so much better than someone like me....a trailer park trash, low-life that was never going to amount to anything. All my life I've been called a nothing, back then all I thought about was being successful in life so I could prove all those people wrong. His words got to me and I made the worst decision of my life. Four days later there I was breaking up with you. I broke things off because at that time, I thought it was the best thing to do."

"Camren, that day I had news to tell you. You remember when I told you that April's father left us?"

"Yes," he said with a nod waiting for her to reveal news that he already knew about.

She turned her back to him. "Ugh, why?"

"Why what?"

"Why after all these years have you come back into my life?"

"Coincidence."

"I believe everything happens for a reason, what's yours?"

"I don't have one, Morgan."

"Faith? Destiny? Is it meant to be?"

"I don't know."

She moved across the room. "You're April's father."

He pretended to be shocked but his expression came out more hurt. "I know." "How do you know?" "The question is why didn't you tell me sooner?"

"I was selfish back then and you fell out of love with me so I didn't want to be with you anymore. I didn't even consider the life that was inside me and then when we graduated I lost contact with you, so I just gave up thinking that we would never see each other again."

"You should've told me," he said as he crossed his arms over his chest.

"I understand if you want to go on about your life," she said after a few awkward moments.

"What?"

"If you wanna go on with life like nothing happened, you can?"

He moved over to her and grabbed her by her shoulders. "What makes you think that I could move on with my life knowing that I have a child? She has my eyes and she plays with her ear when she is tired. That's my kid, why would I give up on the life I created, a life with the woman I love."

She looked up at him in confusion. "What?"

"I'm still in love with you, Morgan. I know you have a boyfriend, but that doesn't change the fact that you were always the one for me. You will forever have my heart." She looked down at the floor. "I don't know what to say."

He went over and gripped her chin making her look up at him. "Say that you understand what I'm saying. Understand that I will now and forever be in my daughter's life, you don't have to do this all alone anymore."

"Ok," she said with a nod.

They embraced each other tightly, she placed her head on his chest and inhaled his scent. A feeling of relief passed over them both, years of secrets being withheld was finally out in the air.

"I'm sorry to cut this moment short but I have to get back to my patients," he said, pulling away from her.

"Oh yeah, of course," she said with a sniffle.

Before leaving her kissed her on her forehead, he stared into her honey brown eyes he had become fascinated with. Then he turned and went back to work with a new feeling overtaking him, a feeling that he couldn't explain.

Camren watched April as she

swung the bat, hitting the ball way into the back field. He loved watching her as she played. She was so passionate about the sport, he was proud to be her father. He remembered the conversation they had at the hospital and her asking him to be her father, now he was able to grant that request for her. He had to make a way for him to see her more often, he couldn't keep going back and forth from Indiana to Denver.

"Glad you could make it," Morgan said to Camren after the game as she approached him by the fence where he stood.

"I told April I would," he said.

"She really loves this sport and she likes when you show up to watch her."

"I love watching her. Glad to see that she's not worried about getting dirty while she's out there."

"She loves softball, she fell in love with it the first moment she was introduced to it. She's not worried about looking like a girl on the field."

"She's got that from you."

She smiled. "No, she gets that passion from you."

"Oh yea?"

"Mmmhm, she gets her talent from me," she said with a smile.

"Yeah, sure," he said with irony.

"Thanks for coming, Mr. Blake," April said as she and a teammate came over.

"No problem," he said.

"Good afternoon, Mrs. Price," April's teammate said.

She had brown hair and a gap between her teeth, her jersey was filthy from sliding in the dirt so much. Her hair was cut short, her eyes from brown and her cheeks were a little on the chubby side.

"Good afternoon, Alice," Morgan said to her.

"I would like to invite April over for a sleepover, do you mind if April attends?" the little girl asked, sounding a bit too old for her age.

"April, do you have clothes packed for this sleepover?" Morgan asked her.

"Yes ma'am, they're in the car."

"And when did you slip that bag into the car?"

"This morning before we left."

Morgan sighed, April had put her in a compromising position. She was a trickster, she reminded him of himself when he was younger.

"Mr. Blake wanted to spend some time with you before he went back," Morgan said.

"I'm sorry, but I really want to go to this sleepover. The whole team is going," April begged.

Morgan rolled her eyes. "Have fun, ask Mrs. White to call me so I can talk to you before you go to bed."

"Thanks, momma," April said as she hugged Morgan around her waist.

"I love you," Morgan said as she hugged her back.

"Love you too," April said as she and the other little girl ran off.

"Girl's will be girls," Camren said as he watched April walk away.

"Yep," Morgan said.

"It's cute to see you worry, she's a tough girl though," Camren said as he turned to walk away.

"Camren," Morgan said.

"Yes?" he said.

"When do you have to be back in Indiana?"

He noticed her fidgeting with her keys. "Not right away, I moved my surgeries to later in the afternoon. What did you have in mind?"

"Want to maybe get something to eat?"

"Would your boyfriend mind that? Matter of fact I've never seen him come to one of April's games."

"We broke up," she said with a frown and a small shrug.

That was great news to him, he played it cool like knowing that she was single didn't excite him.

"That's too bad, he lucked out."

She moved closer to him. "Just stay with me for a couple hours."

"I am kind of hungry," he said, smiling down at her.

They got in his black 2016 Chevy Malibu together, they argued about where they were going to eat. She wanted Ihop and he wanted Longhorn, he knew he wasn't going to win but he wasn't wanting to give in too easily.

He gave in eventually, actually she gave him the silent treatment until he pulled into Ihop parking lot.

She smirked at him since she had gotten her way, he rolled his eyes and then got out to open her door. After eating they went and caught a movie, some horror movie that he wasn't paying attention to because he was too busy thinking about how close she was to him. He actually made a move and wrapped his arm around her, she looked at him but instead of moving his arm she placed her hand on her thigh.

"Thank you for staying with me," Morgan told Camren as they left the movie theatre.

"No problem, I enjoyed myself," he said with his hands in his pockets.

"I have always hated scary movies so I don't know why I suggested going to see it."

She knew exactly why she wanted to see it, so whenever she got scared she could snuggle close to Camren. She had missed being so close to him, she had missed him in general. And when he had slipped his arm around her she was reminded of how much she had missed the smell of his cologne, which he had kept the same for the last seven years, she missed the sound of his heartbeat syncing perfectly with hers.

"Because you know I love them."

"Yeah, maybe that's why."

He opened the car door for her, she was about to get in when she twirled around, grabbed his face and kissed him. His familiar taste clouded her mind, her head was spinning. He pushed her back against his car.

His mind flooded with memories of them back when they were younger, there was still the same intensity as

148

there was back then. He pulled away first and apologized.

She stepped into his space, bringing them nose to nose. "I wanted you to kiss me, Camren, I've been wanting you to since I first saw you at the hospital."

"Really?"

"Yes, you've been so uptight and tense, I just wanted to kiss your stress away."

"But what about Tyler?"

"We weren't serious, he knew that my heart belonged to someone else."

"I should get you home."

She grabbed his arm and pulled him close. "Yeah, we should go back to my place."

He shook his head. "No, I didn't mean like that."

"But I did, please, Camren," she pleaded.

He couldn't say no to her, her hazel eyes just gazing up at him like he was the greatest man on Earth. He held the door open for her, she sighed and then got inside. He drove her to her house, he pulled into the driveway, turned off the engine and then turned to face her.

"Why don't you come inside?" she asked him as she lazily traced a shape on his arm.

He didn't know why but that simple touch had the hairs on his neck, along with other things standing at attention.

"Morgan, are you sure?" he asked.

"Yes, Camren, I'm very sure."

"What if you change your mind in the morning?"

"I doubt I will, but I guess that depends on how well tonight goes."

She moved closer to him, leaning close to his neck. She placed a gentle kiss on him and then another and then another. Camren shivered and then turned to kiss her, the kiss was gentle but very hot. Camren quickly got out of the car, basically ran over to the passenger's side and opened the door for her. They made their way into her house, pulling at each other's clothes and kissing each other with such passion and desperation.

When they were finally in her bedroom, Camren pulled away and took a step away from her.

150

"Morgan, this is my last time I'm asking."

She didn't respond, she just provocatively walked over to him. She placed her hand on the back of his neck and kissed him so deeply he felt it all throughout his body. It was as if that kiss was to show him how she still felt after all these years. He took that as his answer of yes. He scooped her up in his arms and tossed her onto the bed. They made love for hours, built up frustration was expressed through kisses and the closeness of each other's bodies.

♥ Morgan woke up feeling the best she had felt in years. She and Camren had made love for hours, both of them showing how much they had missed out on the years that pasted. She rolled over expecting to feel him next to her but felt nothing. She sat up and looked around, his clothes were not in a pile on the floor anymore. Camren came back into the room fully dressed and he had a frown on his face.

"What's wrong?" she asked. "Nothing," he said plainly. "You look bothered by something

"Uh, nothing," he said as he put on his shoes in a hurry.

"Camren," she said as she swung her legs over the side of the bed.

"It's just that I have this flight in the morning and I'm sure you have an early start tomorrow."

"April won't be back until about 4pm and you can just sleep here and go catch your flight."

"I don't wanna inconvenience you."

She got up, with the bed sheet wrapped around her. She grabbed his arm and he looked at her with weary eyes.

"What happened, Cam, I thought we were good. We just shared a couple hours of passion, did that not mean anything to you?"

"It's not that, Morgan, those hours were incredible but maybe that's what they were. You know? To just remind us of the good times."

"What are you saying?"

"I'm saying that ..."

"So it's just like back in your dorm room, you break my heart and then move on with your life while I'm left to piece myself back together."

"You weren't the only one broken, Morgan," he said, getting upset.

"I think you're forgetting who's leaving right now," she said, getting even more pissed off.

He sighed and ran his hand over his face. "I'm just gonna go back to my hotel. Let me know when April's next softball game and I'll be there."

As soon as he stepped out of her condo instant regret washed over him. "I'm such an idiot," he said to himself as he rode the elevator back down.

He loved that moment they had shared, it brought back old feelings. He just wanted to be with her, to kiss her for hours upon hours, but was he truly over what had happened in the past?

Was he really willing to move past their history in order to reach their future potential?

He left trying to save himself from the sad truth of her rejecting him, she would've told him to leave her place and then things would be weird because he would still want to be with her. He didn't want her to see him beg because that's exactly what he would've done if she had told him to leave.

♥ Camren was having dinner over Kylie's, she and Devin invited him to come over. Morgan was weighing heavily on his mind, he was even too distracted to eat.

"So what's going on with you and Morgan?" Kylie asked Camren as she tossed the salad.

Camren was standing nearby inattentively drinking a beer and Devin was in the living room watching a basketball game between the Lakers and the Bulls. Camren just shrugged at her, not knowing what else to say besides that he was stupid and had seemingly ended all chances of them being together.

"What does that mean?"

"I don't know what we have, she kissed me and ever since I can't get her out of my mind."

She stopped tossing. "Wait, she kissed you?"

"I didn't tell you?"

"No you didn't," she said, placing her hands on her hips.

"We went to go see a movie, after the movie she kissed me."

"She kissed you, did you kiss her back?"

He shrugged again and took a swig of his beer. She shook her head at him and then continued tossing the salad.

"So, what's next?"

"What do you mean?"

"You're the father of her child, she kisses you and then what? Are you two going to end up together? Are y'all going to make up? What about April?"

He shrugged again, she sighed and picked up the bowl.

"I don't know what your problem is, you're a successful doctor, and you have a beautiful daughter and a woman who loves you. Why are you so miserable?"

"Who says I'm miserable?"

"It's evident on your face, it's your attitude."

"I'm not miserable, I just …"

"You're miserable, Camren. You don't date, you just have casual flings with women who you can't see yourself marrying in the near future. Morgan is wanting to start over with you and you're sitting here in my kitchen drinking a beer."

"What do you want me to do? Get on a plane to Denver and get on my knees in front of her and ask her to marry me?"

"No, I want you to admit to yourself that you are in love with this woman, that you still have those same feelings you had for her that you had when you were in college. I remember there was a time when you wanted to quit med school to go get this woman back, find that same person inside you and go after what you want."

He cleared his throat of the emotion threatening to reveal itself. She walked over to him and hugged him.

"What did I miss?" Devin asked as he entered the kitchen on crutches.

"Nothing, onions got to me," Camren said as he wiped his hand over his face.

"Oh ok," Devin said unconvinced.

"Did she ever tell you about how we met?" Camren asked Devin.

"Nope."

"It was actually upon these same circumstances, I was working in a bakery back when I was earning money to pay off my student loans in college. Camren came into the bakery, we were making garlic bread and Camren did not like the smell," Kylie said with a giggle.

"Yeah, I think my eyes started watering," Camren said, laughing as well.

"Sounds like a very memorable moment," Devin said.

"It was," Kylie said.

It wasn't a complete lie, Kylie did work at a bakery and Camren did enter the bakery. But he actually entered the bakery crying, he was upset over Morgan. He had kept replaying the break up in his mind, he was in such a funk. Kylie provided him with a bagel and a nice conversation.

"And you guys have been friends ever since?"

"Yep, couldn't get rid of her," Camren said.

"You love me," Kylie said.

"That's what I led you to believe."

She punched him in his shoulder as they all laughed.

"I got a feeling I'm gonna have a nice speech from you at the wedding," Devin said to Camren.

"I see you're still talking about this wedding," Camren said.

"Yep, and I mean it too. I'm gonna make an honest woman out of her," Devin said as he sat his crutches to the sides. Then he wrapped his arms around her waist.

"And I'll be right there when you do," Camren said.

"I have to finish cooking, why don't you go watch TV with Devin?" Kylie asked Camren.

"I think I might just do that," Camren said.

Camren was in the ER stitching

up a female patient who had cut herself with a knife.

"This is only a few stitches, the nurse will come in and give you specific steps for cleaning and dressing the wound. You should keep the wound and bandages dry, I will give you this ointment to apply to your wound to prevent infection," Camren informed her.

"Thank you, Dr. Blake," she said.

158

"And how exactly did you cut your hand with the knife."

"I was holding an orange in my hand, cutting into it for my daughter when I got distracted. The knife cut into my hand and I had nothing but a dish towel to wrap it up with."

"Ouch, sounds like it hurt."

"It did, never cut an orange like that again."

"You take care," he told her as he stood up and walked away.

"Dr. Blake, phone call," nurse Debra said as she held out the phone to him.

"He took the phone and put it to his ear. "Hello?"

"Hey, Mr. Blake, it's me April," April said.

Hearing her voice on the phone grasped at his heart, to think that less than three months ago he knew nothing of this little girl. And now he's her father. "Hey, sweetheart."

"I wanna go to the park, but mommy is too busy to take me. Can you take me?" "Um, I'm actually in Indiana right now." "Aww," she whined.

"Tell you what, call me back before you go to bed and you can tell me about championships coming up."

"Ok," she said excitedly.

"Then I'll see you whenever I'm free."

"Ok."

"Talk to you later, sweetie."

"Bye," she said. Then hung up.

Camren hung up with a sigh. In that moment he saw his future, he saw him smiling as he held April in his arms, there was a glimpse where he saw Morgan standing nearby watching over with a proud grin.

♥ "Camren, I'm having second thoughts about this," Kylie told Camren as they stood on the front porch to the family house of Devin's mom.

She had invited them all over so she could meet all the people that were important to Devin. She said it had been a while since she had hosted guests and just as long since her baby boy was home for longer than 30 minutes.

"Calm down, Kyles, everything's going to be fine," Camren said as he rubbed up her arms.

"What if his mother doesn't like me? What if I say something that offends her?"

"Then you'll still have a man that loves you and you'll have me by your side. Besides join the club."

She took two deep breaths and then they went to face her soon to be in-laws. They walked through to the backyard, in the back was a whole bunch of family and friends of Devin's.

"Babe," Devin said as he came up to her. He kissed her on the cheek and then put his arm around her shoulders. "Guys this is Kylie, Kylie meet the family."

"Hi," she said with a shy wave.

"You're pretty," a young girl with blonde hair, grey eyes and a barbeque stain in her pink dress said to Kylie. "Thank you," Kylie said as she smiled at the girl.

"That's Samantha, my niece," Devin told Kylie. "Nice to meet you," Kylie said. "I'm Roxanne, her mother," a woman with light brown hair, gray eyes and a humble face. "Nice to meet you," Kylie told her. "This is my best friend, Camren." "Handsome, he has April's eyes," Roxanne said. "Because April is my daughter," Camren said. "Great job, Morgan," Roxanne said as she elbowed Devin.

"Auntie Rox, where's my mom?" Devin asked her. "Last time I saw her she was in the kitchen." "Nice to meet you," Kylie said as she and Camren followed Devin on his crutches as he led the way to the kitchen.

"You too, sweetheart," Roxanne called out after them.

"Ma!" Devin called out.

"In here, honey!" Bethany yelled from the kitchen.

"Ma, I want you to meet Kylie, my girlfriend," Devin introduced her.

His mother sat the crockpot she was holding in her hands down on the countertop, then she turned around, looked at Kylie and smiled a heartwarming smile.

"Hi, I'm Bethany, Devin's mother," Bethany said as she walked up to Kylie with her hand extended.

Kylie shook her hand. "Nice to meet you, I'm Kylie."

"Kylie, that's a pretty name."

"Thank you, I've always liked the name Bethany as well."

Bethany smiled. "Why thank you."

"What all have you cooked, ma?" Devin asked her.

"Well I have some potato salad, macaroni n cheese, macaroni salad, your Aunt Lisa brought in some ribs and her famous dip, Yancy made the cream of corn, your Aunt Roxanne brought some ice cream cake, I have a couple pies in the oven and your father is out grilling some chicken."

"Sounds delicious," Camren said.

"I don't think I got your name," Bethany said to him.

"This is my friend Camren," Kylie said.

"Thank you for having me," he said.

"Thank you for coming, help yourself to any and all food, there's plenty," Bethany said.

"Don't have to tell me twice," he said.

"Ma!" Raymond yelled as he walked through the house. "The prodigal son," Devin mumbled.

"In the kitchen, Ray!" Bethany said.

"Ma, why is Uncle James sitting in my chair? And didn't you get more of that beer I liked," he said as he walked into the kitchen right past Devin, Kylie and Camren and to the fridge.

"Your uncle has a bad back and your father doesn't like that kind of beer, it bothers his stomach."

"He doesn't have to drink it."

"Don't be selfish, son. And speak to our guests."

Raymond finally noticed the other three people in the room. He looked Devin up and down, then he looked at Kylie and smirked.

"It's about time we bring some beautiful women in here," he said.

"Watch it," Devin said defensively.

"Touchy aren't we?"

"This is Devin's girlfriend, Kylie," Bethany said.

"Oh, she's cuter than Tiffany, you remember her don't you Devin?" Raymond asked.

Devin looked at Raymond as if he wanted to smack the smug grin off his face. There was the usual sibling rivalry but with excess tension.

There was some unspoken things needed to be said and with the push of the right buttons and enough liquid courage somebody was bound to let the truth slip.

"I remember her, she was a model wasn't she? She was gorgeous during that one catwalk in Atlanta," Kylie said, surprising everybody with her quick response.

"I didn't really like her, she had a bad attitude but a lovely body," Raymond said. Then he walked back out the room.

"I apologize on behalf of my son", Bethany said.

"Call it like it is, ma, Raymond's a spoiled brat who pouts and mouths off if he doesn't get his way," Devin said.

Kylie reached up and softly touched his jaw. "It's ok."

He took a deep breath. " I'm sorry."

"Why don't yall go back outside with the rest of the family and the food should be ready within the hour," Bethany said.

Camren followed Devin and Kylie out the door back outside. Camren took a seat in one of the empty chairs while Devin introduced Kylie to other family members.

♥ Devin and Kylie were sitting in his rented 2017 silver BMW a couple days later. They had just shared a late night drive after getting doughnuts at a local Krispy Kreme. Devin had her cover her ears as he proved to her that he knew her favorite doughnuts. He ordered two crème-filled doughnuts, one for himself and the other for her. Then he ordered her other favorite which was a chocolate glazed doughnut with sprinkles on top and then half a dozen of the original glazed. She was slightly impressed that he remembered the chocolate sprinkled doughnut, but she had slapped his arm for ordering so many doughnuts, interfering with her nonexistent diet. Devin's phone rang in that moment, it was from his mother.

"Hello," he said as he answered it.

"Honey, where are you?" Bethany asked.

"I'm with Kylie, why? What's the matter?" he asked as he started to worry.

"It's Ray, he's drunk and has gone missing."

"What do you mean missing?"

"I haven't seen him since the other night," she said, sounding practically on the verge of tears.

"Ok, we'll look for him." Then he hung up.

"What's wrong with Ray now?" Kylie asked.

"He's missing," Devin said as he placed her phone back into the cup-holder to rest.

"What do you mean missing?" asked Kylie.

"I mean they haven't seen or heard from him in two days. I'm sorry I need to go look for him.   I think I know where he may be," Devin said.

"You do?" Bethany asked.

He nodded as he pulled out of the parking lot. Kylie nodded even though she didn't have the best feeling about the idea of them being in the same room together. Kylie drove, with the directions of Devin, to an empty basketball court. Raymond stood in front of the basketball goal, just staring up at it as if it was the most marvelous thing in the world. Kylie helped Devin out the car.

"Ray!" Devin called out. "Ray! What are you doing here?"

"Go away," Raymond mumbled.

"Mom and pop have been worried about you, are you drunk?" Devin asked as he moved closer to Devin.

"Why do you assume I'm drunk?"

"Because you're an alcoholic."

"Whatever, just go back to living your perfect life and don't worry about me," Raymond said as he continued to stare at the goal.

"I wasn't worried, your parents were."

"Then you can leave."

"Why can't you just grow up?"

"Devin," Kylie said warningly.

"I am grown," Raymond said as he turned and faced Devin.

"How is living at home with your parents, working at steak and shake, wasting your savings and your parent's savings on alcohol called grown?"

"And how you gonna try to tell me how to live my life, at least I see them unlike you who only come back on Holidays if you even come back then."

Devin handed his crutches to Kylie, then tried balancing on two legs.

"Devin, get back on these crutches," Kylie said as she tried giving the crutches back to him.

"Hit me," Devin told Raymond.

"I don't have time for you," Raymond said as he turned his back on Devin.

Devin pushed Raymond in the back. "Come on and hit me, you didn't have a problem doing it last time."

"Last time was an accident," Raymond said as he got in Devin's face pointing his finger.

"That wasn't no accident, you purposely came down on my legs trying to hurt me. I'm your brother Raymond, your own brother!"

"I said it was an accident!"

"You've given me a hard time ever since we were younger, I used to think you hated me. But then I realized that you hated yourself more than you hated me and you just took it out on me."

"Don't talk like you know me."

"I just wanna know what I did to you."

Raymond just stood there silent, Devin pushed him shouting, "Say it! Say it! Say it!"

"I'm jealous, Devin!" Raymond said as he pushed Devin back.

Devin fell backwards onto the ground since he didn't have the normal amount of balance he usually had with two working legs. Kylie yelped and then ran to Devin's aid. Raymond paced back and forth angrily.

"I'm alright," Devin told her. "Jealous?"

"Yes, you've always been better at basketball than I have, you were my younger brother and you were out doing me. In high school I was known as "Devin's older brother" and I didn't like it, I knew I wasn't gonna amount to anything if I was always compared to you. That's why I made you suffer because I felt like it was all your fault."

"That's how you felt, are you stupid?"

"Don't," Raymond warned Devin.

"I looked up to you, I wanted to be just like you when I was little. I practiced twice as hard on my handles and my shot so I could be just as good as you. Then in high school I was so happy to be on varsity so I could finally play on the team with my big brother, so we could ball out together. But you turned on me when coach started me as a Freshman over you."

"You looked up to me?"

"Yes, I thought you were better than Michael Jordan," Devin said as Kylie tried helping to his feet.

Raymond came over and helped Devin to his feet. "Nobody can be like Mike."

They chuckled together, Kylie relaxed at the gentle sounds of laughter. There was a pause as if they both were thinking.

"I'm sorry," Raymond said so softly it was like a whisper.

"What?" Devin said because he didn't hear him and he didn't remember the last time he had heard Raymond tell him that he was sorry.

"I said I'm sorry, I've acted like a jerk all these years and it wasn't all your fault. I blamed you and held a grudge and I wanna apologize to you."

"I still love you, bro."

They bro hugged and then awkwardly chuckled. Then Raymond noticed Kylie.

"Who's this?" Raymond asked.

"This is my fiancé, Kylie," Devin said as he reached out for her.

She came over to him and they linked hands. She gave Raymond a warm smile.

"She's a beauty, I thought you were dating that short haired chick."

"No, that was my assistant."

"Oh ok, can I get her number?"

"I don't think so."

They smiled at each other and in that moment Devin knew that things had changed between him and his brother and that it would be from now on.

♥ Camren was sitting in the waiting area at the local SOJO's, he had ordered some food to go. He was watching a group of women as they walked by when his phone started to ring. It was Morgan calling.

"Hey, how are you and April?" he asked when he answered the phone.

172

"So you're him? You're April's father," Tyler asked from the other end of the phone.

Camren sat up straight sensing hostility. "Yeah, that's me."

"I just wanna know what took you so long?"

"What do you mean?"

"I mean why all of a sudden are you coming back into her life?"

Camren yelled into the phone. "Because she's my daughter."

"She's been your daughter for the past six years, why all of a sudden have you grown a conscious?"

"You just don't understand."

"I do understand, you're a coward, you leave when she says she's pregnant and then decide after a couple years after everything is all good that you want to come back.

"I didn't know she was pregnant. And I damn sure don't have to explain anything to you."

"I'm not fooled by your doctor degree or your fancy shoes, you're no better than the next deadbeat father."

Camren wanted to say something, he wanted explain himself but he didn't know what to say. How could he explain to a bunch of strangers that he didn't know he had fathered a kid? That the woman he had loved had kept a secret from him for seven years? That the only reason why he broke things off with her in the first place was because he had felt like he wasn't good enough for her and she deserved better.

"What are you doing with my phone?" Camren heard Morgan's voice in the background.

"Here you go, I've said what I needed to say anyways," Tyler said.

"Cam, I'm sorry," Morgan said, getting on the line.

"I have to go," he said as he stood up and made his way to his truck.

He hopped in and drove off without even receiving his food. He didn't know where he was going but driving was keeping him from exploding. His phone rang, he pressed the button on his truck to answer it.

"Camren!" he heard Morgan say.

"Morgan," he said.

"Are you alright? What happened? What did he even say to you?"

"I'm fine," he said bluntly.

"You don't sound fine."

He chuckled to himself, a crazy chuckle and not a funny chuckle. "I just" need to clear my head."

"Where are you?"

"Morgan," he said, wanting her to let it go.

"Where are you?"

He heard her messing with her keys in the background, he didn't want to see her because he didn't know what to say to her.

"Morgan, there's no need to see you, there's no need for any talking."

"Camren, stop it! Now where are you?"

The last thing he heard was her fussing and the sound of the car horn of somebody else's car warning him to stop, then the world went pitch black. In that time he thought about Morgan and April and Mike and how he was such a failure to others. Then he kept hearing his grandmother say, 'You gone be somebody one day, don't let nobody bring you down. If they talk about you let them and then shut them up by proving them wrong.'

He woke up to see Morgan standing by the window looking out into the night. He looked down at himself and saw that he wasn't injured too badly.

"What happened?" he asked in a raspy voice.

"Camren," she said with a gasp as she made her way over to the bed.

He cleared his throat. "Anybody hurt?"

"Only you and that pole you hit,"

He looked down at where her hand was touching his forearm.

"You were distracted and ran into the pole, nobody was hurt or killed. Your main focus should be about healing."

"You're here."

"I am."

"Why?" She sighed and walked back over to the window.

"When the line went dead, I panicked. I thought I was the cause of ... I knew I was the cause of your crash. I couldn't stand losing you, not on the bad terms we left on. You're the father of my child."

"I know this."

"Tyler doesn't know what happened and my father doesn't know, I don't even know the full story!"

"You wanna know why I took that money?"

"Camren," she said as she dropped her head.

He could hear the emotion in her voice, hear the tears begin to well up. "I went to your father to have a man to man conversation about how I felt about you. I had plans to tell him how much I loved you, that I had plans to marry you and I was gonna ask for your hand in marriage. But then he started talking about how I was no good for you and how I wouldn't amount to anything,"

"Oh, Camren," she said as her hand went to her mouth as she cried silent tears.

"Do you know how many times I've heard that in my life? How many times I've heard, 'you're not good enough and you never will be'? Way too many times. I

177

grew up working hard just to prove that I am worth something, that I am more than the helpless, good for nothing little boy abandoned by his mother and father. I did that, I proved myself, I made it to where I am now, and I earned it. I let your father take away one of the best things in my life, I let him get to me.

I took that money he offered me and I went and bought a wedding ring for you, that day in my dorm room I had the ring in my pocket. I hadn't planned on breaking up with you, I was gonna propose to you."

Both her hands were on her face as she cried into them, he wanted to reach out and hold her. He tried to move but his ribs prevented any movement.

"Come here," he told her.

She sat down on the bed and laid her head on his chest, he placed his hand on her head and rubbed it as she cried.

He knew in that moment that being with her was what he wanted most in life. He loved being a well-known doctor and having success, but loving Morgan and April would be one of his greatest accomplishments.

Oh my gosh, Kyles, would you please stop talking about how perfect this wedding is going to be? You're making me sick," Camren said as he sat in the dressing room with her as she was getting her hair and makeup done for her big day.

"If you don't like it, get out," she said.

"Don't mind if I do," he said as he turned towards the door.

"Sit down, don't you dare leave this room or I will kick your-"

"No cursing on your big day," he said with mockery as he walked over to a table that had glasses of champagne sitting on it.

"You cannot be drunk before the reception."

"At this rate you're gonna be begging me to drink in order to deal with you."

"Leave the girl alone, she's in love," Morgan said as she entered the room, looking stunning in her floor-length, strapless red dress and four inch heels.

"I'm just saying, does she have to be overflowing with her love?" Camren asked. Then he took a swig of champagne.

"Would you stop it? It's her day, not yours," Morgan told him as she walked up to him and started messing with his bow tie.

"Yeah, get your own day," Kylie said as she closed her eyes so her people could apply her eye shadow.

He sighed. "Ok, I'm sorry."

"That's better," Morgan said as she kissed him.

"Where's Devin? I know he's walking around stressing everyone out and looking for me," Kylie said.

"He's watching a basketball game," Morgan told her.

"Smart thinking."

Morgan smiled. "Your daughter is asking for you, she won't listen to me. Says that you promised her something special if she tossed the flowers in front of Uncle Devin and Auntie Kylie. Now she won't put on her shoes," Morgan told Camren.

"I got it," he said as he sat his glass down and made his way to where his daughter was located.

"Have you told him yet?" Kylie asked Morgan once Camren left.

"Told him what?" Morgan asked.

"That he has another baby on the way?"

"How did you know?"

Kylie smiled. "I noticed the way you're glowing.

Morgan rushed over to the mirror. "I am?"

"Mhm, you look gorgeous by the way."

"Me? What about you? It's your wedding day."

"I know and Devin has something special planned for our honeymoon if you know what I'm saying," Kylie said wiggling her eyebrows.

"Oh I know, he told me about it."

"He told you?" Kylie said with a gasp.

"I'm his go-to girl, I know everything because I have to book it all."

They both laughed together.

"You should tell him though, he would be really happy to know."

"I'm just-"

"Scared that something is gonna happen before you can tell him?"

"Yeah, because the last time I tried to tell him I was pregnant he broke up with me and I don't want him to leave me again. I mean April loves him so much. But we're adding more to the family, I don't want to scare him off."

"Talk to him, I think he would be excited to be able to be there for the whole pregnancy since he didn't get it with April."

"You think so?"

"You already have one kid with him, so you tell me? But for real, tell him. I mean being with you means the world to him."

"Ok."

Camren went and found April in a room with an adult and a few other kids. She looked so adorable in her dress on, she had her curls in her face.

"Daddy!" April said excitedly as she ran to him.

He scooped her up in his arms. "I heard you won't put your shoes on."

"I don't wanna, I don't like them," she whined.

"But you have to wear them."

"No."

"Come on, April, it's Uncle DJ's wedding. Don't you want to make Uncle DJ happy?"

"Yeah, I wanna see Uncle DJ happy."

"Well good, let's put your shoes on," he said as he sat her down in a nearby chair and helped her put her shoes on.

"You're really great with her," Kathy said as she walked up to them.

"Thank you," Camren said.

"Still can't believe you're her father."

"Me either," he said as he finished tying April shoes. Then he helped her down out the chair so she could play with the other kids.

"I had a feeling, you know, because mother knows best, but y'all had broken up a while ago and the months weren't adding up. I should've known that you were her father, she has your caring spirit and your eyes."

Camren smiled as he gazed at his little girl. "Can't believe I missed out on the first six years of her life."

"Now you have plenty more years to be there for her."

"Yeah, I plan to make up for it."

"Make up for it by being there for all her big moments and the small, show her that you love her and will do anything to protect her and Morgan. Think you can do that?"

Camren nodded.

"Ok everybody it's time," Kylie and Devin's wedding planner, Heaven Reynolds, said as she peeked her head in the room.

"It's time," Camren said to Kathy.

Everybody took the places, the music cued and all Camren was thinking about was his fiancé. Even though this was his best friend's special day, all he could think about was being with Morgan. He looked over at her, she looked so beautiful in her purple bridesmaid dress, and she was smiling hard and trying to keep the tears from flowing. He then looked over at April standing at the back of the church waiting for her cue to start throwing the flowers all over the church. That was his family and he didn't want to lose them, going back and forth between Indiana and Denver.

The next thing he knew he was walking over to where Morgan was standing along with the other bridesmaids.

"Camren, what are you doing?" Morgan asked.

"Yes, what are you doing," Susan, one of the other bridesmaids said with an attitude.

"I came to talk to my fiancé," Camren said as he stared down Susan.

Susan rolled her eyes and stared back down the aisle where everybody else's attention was waiting for Kylie to walk in.

"Fiancé?" Morgan said with a raised eyebrow.

"You better have a good excuse as to why you're out of place, Dr. Blake?" Devin said through his smile.

"This won't take long, I have something I want to say," Camren said.

"Make is fast," Devin said.

"Morgan, I love you," Camren told her.

"I love you too, Cam, but now's not the best time to practice your speech," she said.

"No, this is about us. I was gone for a while and I missed out on a lot of things with you and April. I don't want to miss anything else, I want to be there with you and April for good."

"What are you saying, Camren?"

"Marry me," he said.

She lifted her head up and looked at him with eyes full of tears. "What?"

"Marry me, Morgan, and make me the happiest man on Earth, marry me because I love you so much and I don't ever want to lose you again. Say yes because I know you love me too, just as much if not even more than I love you.

I want to be there for my daughter for the rest of her life, no more wondering who her daddy is, I'm gonna be there for the both of you."

She stared at him for a while, just looking at him in his eyes as if to see if he was for real. Then she finally said, "Yes."

She leaned forward and kissed him, he felt alive again. The pain from the car accident was nothing compared to the love soaring through him at the moment.

"I have something to tell you first," she said.

"Make it quick," Devin whispered.

"Camren, we're going to have another April," she said, touching the side of his face.

His eyes widened. "Really?"

"Yes, I was nervous about telling you-"

"I'm going to be a dad again, I get to be there at the hospital this time?"

She chuckled. "I'm glad you're excited."

"I'm ecstatic, I'm so happy to hear you say that."

"Good," she said with a smile as she felt his arms wrap around her.

"I'm not going anywhere and neither are you," he whispered against her lips.

They kissed again and they both knew that nothing was going to separate them again. ♥

♥ Epilogue ♥

Morgan was having a baby shower for her unborn child, she and Camren were in the process of revealing the sex of their baby and was very excited to find out if they were having a little boy or another girl. Morgan wanted a boy and Camren didn't care as long as the baby came out healthy and had green eyes like him and April. Some of Morgan's friends put the party together and her mom had the props we needed to reveal the gender to everybody.

"How's my niece," Kylie asked as she and Devin entered the house.

"April's good," Morgan said.

Kylie went over to Morgan and hugged her and then kissed Morgan's stomach.

"I was talking about the one you're carrying, it's a girl too."

"Maybe I am, Maybe I'm not," Morgan said with a smile.

"Hey, Morgan," Devin said.

"Hey, Devin," she said.

"Where's the father to be?" he asked as he sat the gift he had brought down on the gift table.

"He's out back with April and the new puppy," Morgan said as she took the plate of deviled eggs.

Kylie took the plate of deviled eggs. "I'll take that."

"What did you guys bring for the baby?"

"We bought the baby a pink basketball," Kylie said as she ate one of the eggs.

"A basketball?" Morgan said as she looked over at Devin.

Devin shrugged. "Just tryna get her started early."

"Who says she's gonna play ball? Or that she's even a girl?" Camren asked as he and April entered the house with the new little brown English Mastiff wearing a yellow collar.

"Hey, Cam," Kylie said.

"Hey, Kyles," he said.

"Cute puppy," she said as she picked up the puppy. "Thanks, her name is Athena," April said.

"Y'all ready to get started," Morgan asked.

"Why can't you just tell us what the gender is already?" asked Kylie as she petted Susan.

"Because I have to pop the balloon first," Camren said as he helped Morgan carry the plates of food outside.

"Who cares? I wanna know now," Kylie said as she and Devin followed them.

"Would you stop pressuring my wife," Camren said.

"Oh shut up. Come on, Morgan, you can tell me" Kylie begged.

They all made their way out back, later on everybody joined the party. Camren's grandparents and a few of his other family members trickled in. Morgan's mother had actually talked Mike into attending, and Melissa was with them. Kylie held the large black balloon as Camren prepared to pop it. The group counted down and then Camren popped it to reveal that they were in fact having …

"It's a girl," Morgan said with a sigh.

Camren and the rest of their guests cheered. Camren kissed her on her cheeks until she finally caved and started celebrating too,

"I told you," Kylie said excitedly.

She put Athena down and then hugged both Camren and Morgan.

"What does that mean?" asked April.

"It means that you're getting a baby sister," Morgan told her.

"Yes!" she said. "That's great because boys are hard to take care of."

They all laughed. Camren looked over at his wife, he was so happy, she was having his second child, and they had a good life. Everything was so perfect.

"I have a name," Camren told Morgan.

"For the baby?" He nodded yes. "Penelope."

"But that's my name," she said with a smile.

"We did say we were gonna name our daughter that." "We did," he said with a wide grin.

She wrapped her arms around his waist. "I love it." Then she kissed him. ♥♥♥

♥Author's Note:

Check My Pulse for Love was a story that I came up with during high school years. I've always wrote stories; however this one was first to be completed.

I was so interested to see how the main characters stories ended. I loved how all of my characters stories played out and wouldn't have had it go any other way.

See Camren and Morgan both were holding back their true feelings in fear of getting hurt. What I would want my readers to get from the story is that honesty is best.

Keep it real with yourself first and then others. You don't want to bypass opportunities and miss out just because you're unsure of how things will turn out.

*You will never know if you don't try, so go for it.

Yours Truly,
   "Bleu Lyric"

♥Author's Bio:

Upcoming African American **Author, Bryanna Foster "Bleu Lyric",** is a 21-year-old college student at The University of North Carolina at Greensboro where she is currently in her junior year majoring in media studies.

She is the second child of four to Bryant and Judy Foster. Born and raised in the small town of Kannapolis, North Carolina, faith in God, education and sports were instilled in her at a very early age

Warm Regards,

Author Bryanna L. Foster

(Bleu Lyric)